CW00688785

DIE FOR YOU

BOOK CLUB BOYS
BOOK 3

MAX WALKER

Edited By: ONE LOVE EDITING

Copyright © 2023 by Max Walker

All rights reserved.

No part of this book may be reproduced in any form or by any electronic or mechanical means, including information storage and retrieval systems, without written permission from the author, except for the use of brief quotations in a book review.

SYNOPSIS

TRISTAN HALL

With a serial killer's crosshairs on my back, the world as I knew it is turned upside down. The threats are real, the fear is palpable, and my survival? Questionable.

Enter Gabriel Fernandez, a hunky detective-bodyguard hybrid with a mission to shield me from danger. Our connection is instantaneous, sparking an undeniable attraction that threatens to melt us both on the spot. But yielding to our emotions could jeopardize my safety, exposing me to danger.

Our solution? Draw a line until the killer is caught, then reassess things then. Except a looming question remains: What if Gabriel fails to stop the murderer in time? And what if our lightning-hot romance only paints a brighter bullseye on my back?

GABRIEL FERNANDEZ

As a detective in Stonewall Investigations' elite division, I specialize in high-stakes cases and perilous pursuits. My latest mission leads me to Atlanta, and straight into the life of Tristan Hall. He's alluring, captivating, and in serious danger.

My task is simple: keep distractions at bay and ensure Tristan's safety while uncovering the identity of the Midnight Chemist. But how can I maintain focus when Tristan himself is the most tantalizing distraction of all?

The stakes are sky-high, and more than just my heart is on the line. As the danger escalates, so do my feelings for Tristan, setting the stage for a case that will change both of our lives one way or another.

ALSO BY MAX WALKER

Book Club Boys

Love and Monsters

Midnights Like This

The Stonewall Investigation Series

A Hard Call

A Lethal Love

A Tangled Truth

A Lover's Game

The Stonewall Investigation- Miami Series

Bad Idea

Lie With Me

His First Surrender

The Stonewall Investigation- Blue Creek Series

Love Me Again

Ride the Wreck

Whatever It Takes

The Rainbow's Seven -Duology

The Sunset Job

The Hammerhead Heist

The Gold Brothers

Hummingbird Heartbreak

Velvet Midnight

Heart of Summer

Audiobooks:

Find them all on Audible.

Christmas Stories:

Daddy Kissing Santa Claus

Daddy, It's Cold Outside

Deck the Halls

———

Receive access to a bundle of my **free stories** by signing up for my newsletter!

Tap here to sign up for my newsletter.

Be sure to connect with me on Instagram and TikTok **@maxwalkerwrites.**

Want more Max? Join Max After Dark.

Max Walker

Max@MaxWalkerWrites.com

1

TRISTAN HALL

THERE WERE a couple of different kinds of phone calls. Some were pleasant, like the calls from an old friend checking in on you. Some were unforgettable, like the FaceTimes that showed off engagement rings or baby bumps.

Then there were the bad calls. The ones in the middle of the night, the sad "hellos," and the tearful "goodbyes." Bad news always ended up being a bitter pill to swallow.

But some calls were downright traumatic. Like the one I had gotten when I was supposed to be in the "happiest place on Earth." A private detective I had reached out to was on the other line, and he was breaking the worst news of my entire life:

I had become the target of a serial killer.

Ever since then, my life changed. Fear commanded my every move. Anxiety gnawed away at me like a living force, feeding off my sleepless nights and restless days. I couldn't write a single word, and for an author staring down the barrel of a hard deadline for a book he'd barely even started—*that* was the stuff of nightmares.

And I was living it.

I must have walked under five ladders, broken ten mirrors, and crossed thirteen black cats because I felt like the unluckiest man in the world.

I dragged myself out of bed and managed to shower and brush my teeth, something that had seemed nearly impossible over the last week. All I wanted to do was stay in bed with the covers over my head, like a turtle tucked away in his shell. I didn't want to deal with anything. Why would I when I could get abducted and killed at any moment?

That was always quite a sobering thought.

Steam still filled the bathroom as I opened the door, the cloud of vapor escaping into the hall. There was a small crack in the mirror that came from the medicine cabinet that was half on the wall and half on the counter. I couldn't really bring myself to fix it, not that I was ever a handyman in the first place. I didn't even want to call someone to fix it.

In fact, I didn't want to make or receive a single phone call for the rest of my (possibly short) life. If it was important, then they could send an email.

My phone started to buzz in my gym shorts. I rolled my eyes and chuckled to myself, taking it out and wondering who was calling me so early in the—

Shit, I thought as I read the time on the screen. *How is it already past noon?*

I answered the call, walking barefoot down the carpeted hall that was in desperate need of a vacuum. Dust bunnies seemed to dance with every step I took. "Hey, Noah, what's up?"

"Did you just wake up?"

"Maybe."

"Tristan, it's almost one o'clock in the afternoon."

"I know, I know. I slept through my alarms." As if I had set any in the first place.

"That's okay. I was just calling to make sure book club was still on for tonight?"

Damn it, that's tonight. "Yes, yup. It's still on. I'll see you guys at seven."

"Okay, and like I said before, my place is still open to host. Jake and I just spent the morning cleaning up, so it's all ready."

I walked into my cluttered living room, a pizza box left open on the coffee table with a couple of crusts still sitting there. Clothes were thrown on the back of the couch, and a pile of unorganized sneakers clustered up next to the door. I stuffed down the sigh that threatened to escape.

"No, it's fine. It gives me an excuse to get things in order over here."

I nearly tripped on an empty Amazon box. I hung up the call and looked around the disaster that was my living room. The curtains were drawn, but the bright late-afternoon sun still managed to shine through, throwing a warm orange filter over the messy space. I pulled open the curtains and looked out to the overgrown front yard.

I couldn't blame all of this on my recent "issue" of being hunted by a psychotic serial killer, although that definitely was a factor.

But if I did some *actual* introspection, I'd realize that this had been building up over the past few years. It was a general sense of unhappiness, a dark and heavy cloud that slowly crept in from the horizon, settling directly above my head and casting everything around me in shadow. I didn't know what had triggered it, nor did I know how to fight it, and it was really fucking my shit up. Not only was the house in a state of disrepair, but I felt my own life falling apart all around me.

My last couple of books didn't do well, my agent dropped me five days before Christmas, leaving me scrambling over the holidays trying to find a new one, my love life was completely and utterly devoid of any joy, and now I couldn't even open up a dating app without being terrified about the faceless person on the other end.

It was shitty. And no one really knew how shitty it actually was. I kept up appearances in front of my friends. I knew none of them had the answers to my problems, and the last thing I wanted to do was worry them, so I kept a smile plastered on and shared whatever shreds of positive news I could find, choosing to ignore the immense sadness that had made residence inside my chest, leeching my hope and creativity with every second that ticked by.

But maybe tonight's book club would help get me out of this depressing mood. We were starting a new book tonight, one I'd been excited about for a while, so at least there was something to look forward to. Plus, I could always count on the Reading under the Rainbow crew to help pull me out of a funk, even if it was temporary.

I got to work cleaning up the living room, tossing shoes into a new pile inside of my closet and bringing the empty boxes to the recycling bin. I looked out the peep-hole before taking the trash to the bin, which was already outside since today was trash day.

Did I bring that out last night?

Possibly. I downed an entire bottle of wine by myself, so a few moments from yesterday evening were slightly blurred out. I walked down my driveway and dumped the bag of trash in the bin. It was a warm summer's day in Atlanta, with the flowers in full bloom and the sunlight beaming down on the cracked pavement. My neighbor's kids were playing tag in the front yard, a floppy golden retriever puppy bouncing behind them as they giggled their way through childhood. It was a cute sight that only made me feel even more jaded. I'd give anything to be running around the yard with my little brother, not a single care in the world except who was winning the game and what we were going to play after.

Back inside, I focused next on cleaning my kitchen. The scent of lemon and lavender from the cleaning spray actually had a calming effect on me, along with the warm water running over my hands as I washed the tower of dirty dishes I had let accumulate.

This wasn't me. It wasn't who I used to be, but I couldn't find my way back. Things just kept falling through the cracks, and it felt like those cracks only kept widening instead of closing.

A noise from behind me made me drop a cup. Thankfully, it was one of the sturdier ones, only making a loud bang but staying intact.

I turned to see a mountain of a man standing under the archway leading into the kitchen, a couple of bags in his hands and an apologetic frown on his stern face. He looked like he had just come from the gym, wearing a black Nike T-shirt and light gray track pants that didn't leave all that much to the imagination.

Gabriel Fernandez. The man who'd come into town wearing a suit of armor, sent to protect me from the monsters that lurked in the shadows. He was a detective from Stonewall Investigations, but that wasn't where his job requirements ended. Once it was determined that the guy I'd been texting with *was* in fact the Midnight Chemist, the owner of the detective agency, Zane, called to tell me he was setting me up with a brand-new kind of detective from their Elite division. Someone who not only had the smarts to crack an impossibly difficult case but also someone who had the muscle and training to act as my bodyguard. It sounded like a solid setup, although I had to admit I didn't think much of it when I initially said yes. There were a couple of things that surprised me, the main one being that I now had a roommate for the fore-seeable future. I'd naively assumed they'd be getting Gabriel a hotel nearby, but with how dangerous my situation was, they had decided that Gabriel staying close was top priority.

Another thing that surprised me? Just how fucking hot my new bodyguard/private investigator/roomie ended up being. It was at least a silver lining, even though Gabriel's looks didn't make up for the lack of words he seemed to possess. The man was a fan of speaking in short sentences without ever divulging anything deep, and trust me, I'd tried. It gets awkward sitting in a quiet living room all evening, so sue me if I end up asking some random questions about Gabriel's biggest fears or worst dates.

"Sorry," Gabriel said, dropping the bags on the kitchen counter. "I called to let you know I'd be out for an hour or so. I had an interview with a possible witness, but that turned out to be nothing. Stopped at the store on my way back."

I glanced at my phone. Sure enough, his missed call was right there. "Shit, I haven't really been paying attention to the phone. Got everything you needed?"

"Yeah, and I picked up the donuts you were talking about yesterday." He opened a bag and pulled out a box of glazed donuts, shining like a first-place trophy in his big hands.

I breathed a sigh of relief and covered my face with a hand, shaking my head. "Gabe, you saved the day. I totally forgot about that."

He gave me a wink, and I nearly toppled over from the sheer force generated by his butterfly-wing eyelashes. "It sounded like you really needed them."

"I did. They're for tonight's game."

"Game?" he asked, crossing his arms and leaning

back on the kitchen island. Gabriel was an ex-Marine and built exactly like you'd expect from a man whose training involved flipping truck tires and running up mountains with weights strapped to their shoulders. He had ox-like shoulders and a strong chest that looked like it would make the most comfortable pillow in the entire world.

"Yeah, drinking game," I explained. "We don't just read books, we also get drunk and read each other."

He cocked his head. "Read? Each other?"

"Yes. Like playfully insulting each other. Have you never—forget it. Just be ready to get that cowlick of yours called out."

Gabriel's eyes opened wide. He put a hand to the back of his head and tried—in vain—to press down the wild swirl of hair. I couldn't help but smile. Something about him was endearing, even though he seemed genetically closer to a brick wall than a human being. He was all knotted muscles and firm jawline and strong brows and big, shiny lips framed by the shadow of a recently shaved beard, and his—

Snap out of it.

I made myself focus on grabbing the box of glazed donuts. Truth was, Gabriel was exactly my type. Tall and muscular and a little rough around the edges, just enough to make him interesting but not to cut anyone getting too close. This was only his second week living with me, and he was already picking things up for me at the grocery store, something that I doubted was listed under his responsibilities, but he still did it anyway.

But I wasn't in the position to even *think* about dating

anyone. I had to look inward before I started gawking outward. Besides, he was here to do a job, not to date me. I couldn't just assume he wanted me as badly as I wanted him, and I wasn't in the mental state to deal with rejection.

Nope. Not happening.

"Alright, I'm hopping in the shower," Gabriel said, peeling off his socks and bundling them in his hand. My eyes dropped to his feet for a moment. Sexy, well taken care of, perfect just like h—

Ah fuck, this is gonna be hard, isn't it...

2

GABRIEL FERNANDEZ

I GOT INTO THE BATHROOM, dropped my shorts, and took off my shirt before turning on the shower, making the water steaming hot as I stepped inside.

When my good friend Zane called to tell me about a new job offer he had, I said yes before he even finished explaining. I'd been in a rut. I worked as a private body-guard, and before that, I did a short stint as a police offi-cer. I was having trouble figuring out what the fuck I wanted to be doing in my life, so Zane's offer came at the perfect time.

I packed up my bags and moved to New York City, where his agency was headquartered at.

I spent two years training with him alongside the other guys he had brought in for his new "Elite" division. Zane was one of the best detectives in the business. Learning under him gave me the confidence I needed to take on Tristan's case. I'd already worked a few others before this (saving a famous actor from an unhinged stalker, protecting a senator after he received some horribly homophobic threats), but Tristan's case felt like it had the highest stakes yet. If I could keep him safe and solve who the hell was behind these killings, then I could be saving more than just one life.

It wasn't going to be easy, though. Not at all.

I'd already met with local law enforcement and tried to get everything they had on the case, which amounted to a whole stack of nothing. Next, I went to the FBI, an organization that wasn't exactly well-known for being open and forthcoming with what they had.

It was another dead end. Frustrating but not case-ending. I would just need to start from scratch. So I compiled a list of the victims first and tried to pull a common thread through them: all of them were gay, not all of them were single, some were women and some were men, and each one was found to have died at exactly midnight from being injected with a rare and complicated mix of deadly chemicals. The victims were then placed in the bathtub with the sink faucet left on. An odd touch that appeared to be some kind of calling card from the killer, but why?

The only solid lead was a phone number we were able to connect to a Grindr account. When Tristan started getting weird vibes from the person on the other side of his yellow and blue chat bubbles, he reached out to Zane, and we were able to link the phone number with the account. Unfortunately, the number was on an untraceable burner phone, so we couldn't use it to hunt the killer down, but it did give us the ability to go into the account and read through the messages.

Sure enough, all of the past victims were on there, along with many who stopped talking to the killer right before meeting up with them, unknowingly saving their own lives by ghosting the account. It wasn't easy to read through, knowing that six of these people were now dead because of these very chats, but it was necessary. I went through that account with a fine-toothed comb, analyzing the way the killer spoke, trying to pick out any little details that might help me figure out who was behind this.

I pumped a handful of the coconut shampoo into my palm and soaped up my hair, dipping my head back and letting the water wash it all away, warm beads dropping down my back and easing some of the sore muscles in my back after this morning's workout. I could hear Tristan walking past the bathroom, laughing at some dumb video he had pulled up on his phone.

When I'd taken this case, I hadn't prepared myself to meet a man with a golden smile and a charming wit, two things that I was very attracted to. It absolutely didn't hurt that Tristan had plenty of other qualities that I was attracted to: his big hands, his perfect teeth, his nice lips, his sexy legs, his suckable toes, his—

Fuck. Thinking of my charge just outside the bathroom door made my cock twitch. I ran a soapy hand over my hardening length.

Tristan was the kind of guy I stayed away from, only because he was the kind of guy I knew could destroy me if I let him. And I didn't let *anyone* close enough to wield that kind of power over me. That's why I liked having a handful of no-strings-attached hookups I could reach out to whenever I needed to blow off some steam. Keeping my dick separate from my emotions made my life easy. I'd seen firsthand what kind of trauma and pain a relationship gone wrong could inflict, so I decided at a pretty young age that I never wanted one to begin with.

I shook off the chill that climbed up my spine, battling with the warmth of the water. I continued to fist my now fully stiff cock. I squeezed around the head, slowly traveling down to the base, imagining my hand as Tristan's instead. I shut my eyes and leaned against the wall, opening my legs, my grip getting tighter. I couldn't let him close, so I had to make sure I wasn't a horny mess the second I stepped out of the bathroom.

I had to let go. I had to empty my balls. I palmed them as they pulled up toward my body. A low sigh escaped my lips as I picked up the pace, jerking off faster, feeling my core tighten as my release came rushing toward me.

I bit my lip and blew, come shooting out onto the glass screen, mixing with the water and sliding down into the shower. I sucked in a deep breath, my body shivering from the momentary blast of pleasure and endorphins.

There. Now I could look Tristan in the eye and not worry about lust turning me feral.

At least for the next few hours.

I finished washing up, my still-swollen cock dripping as I stepped out of the shower. I grabbed my towel from off the wall and ran it up and down my body. Tristan's bathroom wasn't exactly the most organized and definitely needed a good deep cleaning, but I wasn't about to tell him that. It seemed like he was already wilting under the pressure that came with being the target of a sadistic serial killer, along with whatever else he had going on in his life, and I didn't want to add on to that in the slightest. My job here was to protect Tristan and to figure out the identity of this Midnight Chemist. Nothing more and nothing less.

But... well, I could at least wash the sink and toilet while I was in here. I crouched down and dug through the half-empty bottles of cleaning supplies he kept under his sink. I grabbed the Lysol and a scrub and got to work.

After about thirty minutes, Tristan's bathroom looked brand-new. It smelled like lemon Pledge and bleach. I pushed open the small window that was above the toilet to let in some fresh air.

This may not have been part of my job description, and I typically hated having to get on my hands and knees to clean behind a toilet, but I had to admit it felt good knowing I'd helped him out a bit. There was something about Tristan that made me want to see him smile twenty-four seven. I'd realized it pretty quickly after meeting him. It was the way an entire room seemed to light up when he flashed those pearly whites. That smile should never be tamped down.

I finished getting dressed, putting on a black tank top and gray basketball shorts. My hair was no longer wet, allowing me to mess it up a bit.

Outside, I could hear Tristan watching TV in the living room. He greeted me from the couch, lying down with his feet on a pillow and his focus turning back to his phone.

"I thought you drowned in there for a second," he said, his eyes floating back to me and lingering for a moment.

"I'd make a pretty shitty bodyguard if I drowned in your shower. Just staring up at the shower-head with my mouth open."

Tristan chuckled. "Turkeys do that, you know. They'll look up at the rain with their beaks open and end up swallowing too much."

"Good thing I'm not a dumb bird, then." I went over to the love seat and plopped down. "I was just cleaning up in there."

Tristan shot up on the couch, nearly dropping his phone. "What? Seriously?"

I nodded and looked at the television, trying to keep my smile down. He looked so surprised. I kind of liked throwing him off like that.

"Oh, that's so embarrassing," he said, standing up and walking down the hall to the bathroom. He came back, looking shocked, his hands in the pocket of his khaki shorts. A silver bracelet glittered on his wrist, matching the silver necklace that peeked out from the collar of his shirt.

"Gabriel, you really didn't have to do that." He shook his head. Were those tears in his eyes? Before I could take a closer look, he turned away.

"It's fine. I don't mind cleaning up sometimes."

"I just... thank you." He wiped at something on his cheek and disappeared into the kitchen. I decided to give him some space, not realizing how emotional cleaning his bathroom would make him. I knew Tristan was a writer, which likely meant he was a highly sensitive soul, but this reaction surprised me.

Huh...

I tried not to focus on it. Tried not to think about what other surprises Tristan had for me. I instead unlocked my phone and went to the folder that held my case files. There wasn't such a thing as downtime for me. This job was a twenty-four-seven kind of commitment, and I was determined to see it through.

3

TRISTAN HALL

I NEARLY BROKE DOWN. Seeing my bathroom sink shining and the mirror sans any toothpaste spots meant more to me than if someone showed up at my door and randomly said I won the lotto. It wasn't only an unexpected gesture, but it was also the sweetest damn thing anyone had ever done for me. And it was done by a man who used words with the same frequency as a boulder. A man built like one, too. One who was sent here to protect me, not to look after me... but he did. He took his time to make the bathroom look brand-new after I'd been neglecting it these past few weeks.

Thankfully, I held it together until I was able to escape into the kitchen, where I leaned on the counter and stuffed a knuckle in my mouth to stop my crying from being audible.

What was going on with me? I tried to swallow down the bubbling emotion, but that only made it push up my throat with even more force. I shut my eyes and tried to calm myself down, realizing that it wasn't just the clean bathroom that I was crying about now.

I was crying for the life I used to live. Before I'd become the target of a serial killer. Before my books started to nosedive on the charts. Back when I used to be happy. Used to be able to go out and meet a guy, have a good time, make a solid connection and some great memories. When I was able to hang out with my friends, reading our silly little books and drinking our silly little wine, having just a silly little time.

All of that was gone. The Midnight Chemist may not have gotten to me (yet), but they'd effectively killed off any hope I had of being happy. At least for now. It just didn't seem like something I was even capable of anymore, which was why the bathroom made me even *more* emotional. Gabriel gave me a gift he didn't even know I needed: he made me feel *happy* again. It was the tiniest spark of light in the all-consuming darkness that surrounded me, but damn it, I felt it. And I didn't want to let it go.

I pulled myself together and grabbed an empty cup from the cupboard, going to the fridge and pressing it up against the ice dispenser. The clink of ice against glass filled the kitchen, replaced by the sound of running water. I took a sip, letting the cold drink ground me. It helped me focus on something other than the tidal wave of crap currently washing over my brain.

A deep sigh left me as I put the glass down. I should probably use this energy and channel it into something good. I could go to my office and lock myself in until I managed to get some words down on a page. No matter how shitty they might be, I just had to sit down and *write*. But one quick glance at the clock shot down any hope of that happening.

Somehow, the day completely slipped by me. And although Gabriel did a wonderful job of cleaning my bathroom, there was still the rest of the house that I had to deal with, and there were only a couple of hours left until book club started.

I began to regret my choice of pushing hard to host tonight's meeting. I wanted to do it because I needed to hold on to a sense of normalcy now that everything else around me was spinning out of control. I needed to be surrounded by friends, in a space that felt safe for me. I knew that I was the sole target of the Midnight Chemist —they'd made that clear with their last message to me, those words seared into my being like a brand on a bull: *You're mine. I've never craved someone as badly as I do you, Tristan. You're mine. You're next.*

It was the message that triggered me into reaching out for help, and the one that helped Stonewall Investigations link the Grindr user to the serial killer.

AnemoneUnderSea was actually the Midnight Chemist, and I had sent that motherfucker a damn face pic. Thankfully, I didn't send him more than that, but still, he knew who I was and knew the distance I'd been from him when we started chatting. It was enough to put the pieces together.

So being surrounded by people helped. Especially when one of those people was Gabriel Fernandez, bodyguard extraordinaire and the detective of my dreams.

He'd actually suggested keeping the book club at my place when I asked. He said it would be easier to secure since he already knew my house like the back of his hand. He'd do a couple of laps around the property during the night just to make sure there wasn't anyone lurking in the bushes. He assured me that we'd all be safe, and when Gabriel drops his voice and his words turn to pebbles in a streaming riverbed, smooth and pleasant with a vibration that settled down into your chest, then you believe every damn word that comes out of his mouth.

I gulped down the rest of the water and collected myself before going back out into the living room, where Gabriel was already wiping down the coffee table.

Jesus, did I get a bodyguard or a professional cleaner? I honestly didn't mind the combo at all, but I certainly wasn't going to let Gabriel keep working. I rushed over and snatched the rag from his hand. "Uh-uh," I said, shooing him away. "Go do detective stuff or something. I've got the rest of the cleaning."

Gabriel cocked his head, looking at me like he was trying to study me. I licked my lips and dropped my eyes down to the table. It was difficult being in the same room as this Adonis and not picturing a kiss. He had the kind of magnetic pull that—well, that I usually reserved for the heroes in my novels. But this man was standing right in front of me, inches away from me. I could reach out and touch him if I wanted to... and trust me, I did. From the moment we met, I knew Gabriel would be trouble, even though he'd been sent here to be the exact opposite.

"I do have a few phone calls to make. I'll go to the guest room so I don't bother you."

"That's totally fine. I wouldn't mind some background noise. And your voice is actually really soothing."

"Is it?"

I looked up from the coffee table, realizing Gabriel had moved closer to me. "It is." I swallowed, nearly making an audible gulp. The air in my house suddenly got about twenty-five degrees hotter. Did the fireplace turn on by itself? The heater?

"Guess that's why I did such a great job that time I worked as a telemarketer."

I arched a skeptical brow. "Seriously? I can't imagine you sitting behind one of those ancient computers with a headset on."

"Well, try harder. It was my first job out of high school. Only lasted a couple months before I went into the military, but I made a nice amount of commission from it. And a few propositions for a more X-rated call." Gabriel's cocky smirk nearly knocked me over.

"That's, uh, very interesting." I couldn't really form words. Ironic, considering my career was built on doing exactly that. I swallowed again, this gulp much louder than the last.

Gabriel chuckled and grabbed his phone. He went to the couch and sat down, leaning forward so his broad shoulders pushed against the fabric of his thin T-shirt. "If I do end up bothering you, just tell me and I'll move."

"I'll poke you, how about that?"

"I might end up liking that," he said, not looking up from his phone, but I could still hear the smirk through his tone.

I didn't respond. I turned my attention back to cleaning and not to the rapid beating of my heart or the sweat that had started to form at the base of my neck. Was Gabriel flirting with me? And was it okay if I did it back? I wasn't entirely sure if there was a rule against hooking up with clients.

I was getting ahead of myself. My romance-starved brain was simply latching on to the littlest things. Thirsty. That's exactly what I was, and not in the way that would be helped by the glass of water I drank earlier. This thirst went a little deeper.

The rest of the house wasn't too bad. A quick surface wipe down and some rapid-fire organization attempts made the mess move from the living room to my closet floor. Laundry could be done later, even though the overflowing hamper was beginning to scare me.

Still, I managed to finish up about thirty minutes before the first people started to show up. It was just enough time to pop open a beer and sit on the couch, where Gabriel and I scrolled through a feed of funny videos, sharing the ones we liked most with each other. It was interesting because his account had much more content around the military and cars, which were two of his bigger passions, but he did have some solid comedians that he followed, all of them either women or gay, which were the only comedians I normally found funny in the first place.

The doorbell rang as I showed him a video of the newest dance move. "You're learning it with me," I said as I got up to answer the door.

Noah and Jake stood on the other side, Jake holding up a bottle of Veuve champagne, the pink wrapping serving an instant serotonin hit. Steven was also with them, having hitched a ride with the smiley couple.

"How you feeling?" Noah asked after we broke from our hug, swapping Noah out for Steven. His hugs were also so tight and warm. Some people just knew how to hug, and Steven was one of them, his hands pressing tight against my upper and lower back.

"Good. Better now that you guys are here." I welcomed them in, trying not to take a prolonged look out to the street. It was just a regular night, with the neighbors all home and my driveway beginning to fill up with cars. My house was located right in the center of a cul-de-sac. There weren't many places to hide if someone was in fact watching me.

"Safety in numbers," Jake said as he walked in and shrugged off his coat. "I've seen enough nature documentaries to know that."

"Still doesn't stop the lion from picking off the weakest one," I rebutted.

"Well, that's probably good news for you, then," Noah said. "We all know I can't run for shit. You'd smoke me."

"I wouldn't leave you behind," I said, nudging my

friend with a shoulder. "I already saved your life once. I think I could do it again."

"Touché," Noah replied. He shot me a wide grin and went with Jake to the kitchen to grab drinks. They greeted Gabriel with warm hugs as they crossed paths in the living room. He'd already met most of my close friends, but tonight, he'd be meeting the entire book club, and we'd grown pretty steadily over the last few months. I had to bring chairs in from the garage to fit us all for tonight's meeting.

It didn't take long for the rest of the crew to arrive. We settled in with our drinks and our books, and the laughter quickly filled the air, my friends able to lift my spirits in a way that was very much needed.

Too bad none of us knew just how bad things were about to get.

So much for it being a regular night.

4

GABRIEL FERNANDEZ

I JUST FINISHED DOING a lap around the house, coming back into the living room, where a lively discussion about penis size was going on. I would have been surprised if it hadn't been brought up right before I left. Apparently, the book everyone was reading had to do with a man who was deeply ashamed of something, but the reader wasn't made aware of what. There was also a killer on the loose, who seemed to be targeting the main character *because* of whatever the man had been ashamed of. It had been Yvette who suggested it: "What if he's just got a monster dong?"

The room had burst into laughter and apparently got hung up on this man's hang-up because they were still talking about it when I sat back down. I noticed Tristan shoot a glance in my direction. I gave him a reassuring nod and a smile, which seemed to ease some of the tension coiled up in his stiff shoulders.

The group was arranged in a rough semicircle in Tristan's spacious living room. There were pillows on the floor, where some sat cross-legged while others took up space on the couch. A pile of snacks sat in the center of the group, with the donuts I had brought earlier nearly wiped out. Tristan leaned forward and grabbed a half-empty bottle of champagne, filling up his glass.

"I don't know," he said, attention turning toward him. "I think big dicks are actually really nice. Like there's a beauty to them."

I straightened my back and tried to ignore the flush of heat that spread through my core, as if someone flipped a switch inside me.

What the hell conversation did I just come back into?

And why does Tristan talking about big dicks turn me on?

Noah scoffed at that while Eric nodded his head. Those two were apparently the core of Tristan's friend group, having been best friends since back when they were kids. Tia, Jess, and Yvette were also close to Tristan, from what I gathered, but the others were all either plus-ones or relatively new members of the friend group. Evan Wilson was the newest addition. He was Yvette's boyfriend and seemed to be a man of very few words, having only spoken a couple of times throughout the night. Was he possibly being the only straight guy in the group making him uncomfortable?

"I've gotta agree," Eric said. "Bigger is usually better. Trust me." He gave a wink at his fiancé, Colton, and kissed him on the cheek.

"Of course you size queens are agreeing," Tia said

with an arched brow. "But I don't think our character is thinking about peen size, okay? I think he's ashamed of the fact that he wants to kill. I think the main guy is the actual killer."

Heads swiveled in Tia's direction. She sat at the edge of the couch, an arm thrown casually on the back of the couch, the open book full of highlighted notes sitting on her lap. "Really?" Jess asked, moving her feet from under Tia's legs and sitting up straight.

"Is that an official guess?" Tristan asked. He raised his glass. "Remember the rules for tonight."

"Right," Tia said as she leaned forward to grab her drink. "I, Ms. Tia Sherlock Holmes-to-Go, want to put in a guess."

The group chuckled as Noah announced Tia's name again, welcoming her to the stage.

It was the game Tristan had come up with. If anyone wanted to make a guess as to the killer and their motive, then they'd have to first come up with a detective-themed drag name and lip-sync to a song, *or* they could pass on the lip-sync and take a chug of their drink instead. Apparently, he was a fan of drag queens and promised he'd take me to a show at some point, nearly being knocked over after I told him I had never been to a drag show before.

I tried not to pay attention to how excited that made me. I was beginning to find that any time spent around the intriguing and handsome writer was time *extremely* well spent.

Tia chugged her champagne and wiped her lips with

the back of her hand, smiling. The book they were reading was called *Twisting Razors*. "Okay, but seriously, look at the way the chapters from the killer's perspective are written—they seem very similar to Kenneth's chapters. And there's the whole mystery about all those cats dying around Kenneth as a kid. I think that's because he was killing them."

"That actually... could be true?" Jake said, looking down at his book. He wore gray sweatpants and a black T-shirt, which was the exact opposite of what his husband wore: black short shorts and a gray long-sleeved shirt. "I wrote down that possibility, too."

"But that's pretty ballsy on the author's part," Steven said. He was sitting on the floor with his back against the couch, legs crossed underneath him. Tristan had told me he was one of the newest members of the Reading Under the Rainbow club, having bumped into Eric in their apartment's hallway when Eric passed on the invite.

"To have us follow the murderer?" Tristan asked.

"Exactly," Steven said. He glanced down at his phone and tapped at the screen before leaning over and touching Tristan's ankle. "Sidebar, but what's the Wi-Fi password?"

"Hold on, let me show you," Tristan said as he got up from the couch and went over to the router, which was inside the sleek white entertainment center. "I always have a suspicion that if I read these sequences of letters and numbers out loud, then I'll accidentally open up a gate to Hell."

That got a collective laugh out of the group. The

smile pulled up at my lips, feeling almost foreign after setting them in a frown for so long. It was refreshing to see a group of friends gathered around and shooting the shit. I'd been missing that in my life lately. All of my close friends were scattered across the globe, working different jobs or settling down with different people. A couple of texts every few months to reassure us that the other was alive was all I got. I never had a home base where I could plant me and my chosen family down, but Tristan clearly did, and that made me happy for him.

It was also good to see him smiling so much. I'd been here for a few weeks now, and his smile—as beautiful as it was—had felt very elusive. And I didn't blame him. He must have had a mountain of crap on his mind, so I never expected him to walk around with a fake smile plastered on his face.

Still, seeing the real thing was nice. I decided I wanted to see it more often from here on out.

"Thanks," Steven said, "I'm connected."

"Do you have to keep up with your Grindr dates? Don't want the nudes taking up your data?" Noah teased.

Steven's cheeks didn't change color but the way he shrunk back into his seat said he had some shyness to him. "I might be deleting that app soon."

"Oh, found someone worth deleting it for?" Jake asked.

"Possibly. But I don't like to jinx things." He looked down at his lap, tapping his nails against the cracked plastic blue of his phone case.

"Well invite them next time," Tristan said as he took

his seat. I was leaning against the far wall with a clear view of the front door, but I was having a difficult time taking my gaze off Tristan. He had on a pair of khaki shorts that bunched up as he sat down, his smooth, muscular thighs on full display. He was barefoot, with the soles of his feet aimed at me as he crossed them at the ankle. They were at least a size eleven, which made me wonder what else he was above average with in terms of size?

"Alright," he continued off Steven's silent nod, "I think we can start wrapping up tonight's book club there. Let's see if Tia's guess about Kenneth being the killer is right *or* that his shame has something to do with his donkey dick."

More laughter spread through the room. Everyone seemed to be having a great time, regardless of the threat that Tristan was under. He needed this. They all did.

Well, maybe not all of them. Evan Wilson didn't seem to be having much fun at all. He had his arms crossed against his chest and his gaze turned down toward his feet. Yvette appeared to be trying in vain to get him to participate, whispering something in his ear and rubbing his back. Nothing seemed to be pulling Evan out of his shell.

He stood up abruptly and went down the hall to the bathroom. Yvette mouthed out, "Sorry," to the group. Tristan put up the music a little louder and leaned forward.

"Is everything okay?" he asked, clearly having picked up on Evan's mood.

"Yeah, I just think he has anxiety around big groups. He warned me about it, but I didn't realize he'd shut down like that."

"That's okay," Tristan said. "As long as you like him, then we like him."

Yvette smiled and appeared to be on the cusp of saying something else but quickly stopped herself as Evan came back into the room. Everyone acted as though nothing weird had just occurred, with Noah and Jake standing up first to collect the trash, Eric joining them while Colton got into a heated debate with Jess, Tia, and Steven over the perfect pizza toppings.

I figured another lap around the property likely wouldn't hurt. It was a quiet neighborhood with plenty of outdoor lighting and well-manicured open spaces, meaning there weren't a lot of places to hide. Still, it was part of my job duty, and I wasn't about to let anything slide on this one.

Just as I reached the front door, the music abruptly cut off, and the television clicked on with a cheery chime. I paused, looking for who had the remote but seeing everyone else just as confused. Tristan went over to the coffee table and picked up the remote, clicking it, and nothing happened. He cocked his head.

"Huh, must be a glitch or something," he said.

The screen flickered and filled with camera footage filmed sometime in the middle of the night. I, along with everyone else in the room, immediately recognized the scene that filled the screen.

"That's my front lawn," Tristan said, confirming it for

anyone who might not have guessed. "It's my Ring camera, but I never connected it to my TV like this?"

"Everyone move away from the windows and doors," I said, my words dropping in the room like a bomb. Tristan looked at me with wide, fearful eyes.

"It's a bug, right? Let me see if I rest—"

"Oh my God," Noah said, pointing at the screen. "Look."

A shadow appeared on-screen. A wraith cutting across the lawn. A person dressed in all black, a ski mask covering their face, and a long and bulky black trench coat hiding their figure. The shadow walked down the stone path, a confidence in their strut with a hand in the pocket of the coat.

I went for the concealed gun strapped in my holster and whipped it out, raising it up toward the door. Someone behind me yelled, the piercing screech cutting past the sound of blood pumping into my skull.

"No one move," I said as my eyes dropped to the knob. Maybe the fucker didn't know there was a six-foot-three bodyguard waiting with a gun on the other side of the door. And if they didn't?

Well, they were about to find out.

5

TRISTAN HALL

MY WORST NIGHTMARE was coming true. This sick fuck was about to walk through that door, expecting to grab me but instead walking face-first into Gabriel's gun. Jess and Tia were pressed up against the wall, with Noah and Jake on their left, all four of them looking terrified out of their minds. Yvette was on the floor being shielded by her boyfriend while Colton, Steven, and Eric were each holding items to use as a defense. I wasn't sure where Steven got that knife from so quickly, but I was slightly grateful for it.

Did the doorknob just jiggle? It was locked, but could this person force it open? Would they?

I looked to the television screen. The night-vision filter was on, casting my front lawn in an eerie white shade. Like footage from a ghost hunter's vault. But...

The video was on a loop. My stalker was walking back down the path, just like he had moments before. He reached the door, worked the lock for a moment, and then he opened it, stepping inside. I hadn't seen that part earlier.

"Wait," I said, surprised my vocal cords still worked. "This is an old video."

"Huh?" Gabriel asked over his shoulder, his attention pinned to the front door.

"It's not from tonight. Look, none of your cars are there. This was done some other night." My stomach twisted even tighter as realization set it. "They were in here. The Midnight Chemist was inside my house while I slept."

My knees started to tremble, but I managed to get them working enough to carry me toward the kitchen sink, where I threw up from the raw fear.

Eric and Noah appeared at my side. My best friends. My boys. We were supposed to be enjoying our late twenties together, going to bars and movies and weddings and triple dates. We'd already been through so much together, and now this?

"Gabriel is going around the perimeter," Eric said, his hand rubbing the spot between my shoulder blades as Noah poured me a fresh glass of ice water.

"He was in here," I said. It felt like a bucket of spiders had been dumped over my head. A thousand invisible and tiny legs were crawling against my skin, down my spine, inside of my chest. This was a kind of fear I had never known before. I looked around my kitchen, not trusting a single inch of my own home. As if he were crouched in my cupboard, waiting until I was alone to crawl out and have his way with me. "He came in here while I slept."

I leaned back over the sink as my stomach did a summersault, but nothing came out.

"Maybe this video is going to be what reveals their identity," Noah helpfully suggested, although I could hear the fear cause his words to tremble.

"Noah's right," Eric said, his voice a little more steady. I stood up and leaned against the sink, looking at my best friends washed in the orange light of my kitchen, their expressions revealing the thoughts they didn't want to say out loud. "They might have gotten too confident. Is there a way you can see how that video got on your television?"

I huffed a breath. My lungs felt like they could hold a fraction of the air they were supposed to. "I might be able to. 'Might' being the key word."

Writing wasn't my only passion. Since I was a kid, technology always had a vise grip around my interests. I loved tinkering with codes and computers, learning an entirely new language that I'd likely never be able to use in my books but that I'd used plenty of times otherwise. I could possibly see where the hell that video came from, but it was going to take some time and mental capacity to pull off, neither of which I felt like I had in the moment.

Gabriel came into the kitchen, concern twisting his normally neutral expression. He filled up the doorway, his broad shoulders nearly up against his earlobes with how tense he must have been.

"Anything?" I asked, already knowing the answer.

"Nothing." Gabriel came over to me, and for a second, I felt like he was going to reach out for my hand, but he veered off at the last moment and grabbed an empty cup from the clean side of my sink. He poured himself some water, gulping it down like someone who'd just been saved from the desert.

"I feel sick. Violated." Another shiver shot down the center of my back.

"That's exactly what he wants you to feel," Gabriel said. "And that's exactly why I'm getting us an Airbnb to stay at. It's no longer safe here."

I tried to take in another deep breath, but all that managed to sneak past my tightening chest was a wisp of air. I let it out with a rattle. "This is my house. It's one of the only things I have to my name. I can't... I can't let him win."

"It's not about winning or losing right now." Gabriel's blue eyes held a growing storm in them. It was as if I were seeing the lightning clap against the sky on the distant horizon, hearing the thunder roll in moments later. "It's about keeping you safe."

His jaw twitched, the lines that formed his silhouette growing even sharper.

"Gabriel's right," Eric said. "It's not safe here. Not right now."

The sick feeling in my stomach began to disappear, replaced instead by a sudden and intense sadness. "Why? Why is this shit happening to me?"

Gabriel did reach across the distance that separated us this time. His hand landed on my elbow, squeezing gently, his thumb making tiny circles as his stormy blue eyes worked as lighthouses leading me back to shore. "There isn't always a reason for everything, Tristan. Random chance created the universe, and random chance drives our lives. Trust me. The shit I've seen as a Marine and then as a detective, it makes me realize life just isn't fair, not to anyone. Sometimes the dice lets you walk away with the bank, and sometimes it wipes you out.

"But, and this I *do* know, chance always comes back around in your favor. You just have to keep playing the game. You can't give up."

His words landed with a sharpness that cut through some of the brain fog currently eating away at my thoughts. He was right. There was nothing I could do in this moment but keep going, keep fighting. And something about Gabriel's hand still on my elbow helped make that idea even stronger. I was able to take in a deep breath, shaking out the tension in my shoulders with the exhale.

"Okay, let's get everyone out of here safely, and then I'll pack, and we can go."

Gabriel nodded, his blue eyes scanning me as if searching for any sign of physical harm. Like he wasn't just my bodyguard but my doctor, ready to tend to any wounds.

Unfortunately for me, these wounds were the invisible kind. The ones that were the hardest to treat. I looked to Noah and Eric, both of whom appeared stoic, even though I could tell the fear hadn't spared them, either. Noah fidgeted with his bracelet, and Eric was rolling his fisted hands in a circle, both telltale signs that my best friends were anxious, and they had good reason to be.

The rest of the night became a blur. We decided to have everyone leave all at once and to take the long routes home, just in case they picked up any unwanted tailgaters on the way. I had everyone call me the second they arrived back to their place, gratefully answering their calls as I rushed around my bedroom, tossing clothes and device chargers and toiletries all into one big suitcase. It started to hit me as I zipped the overflowing suitcase up, realizing that this wasn't me packing for a trip to London or the Bahamas—this was me packing so that I could run for my life.

And being back in my bedroom... knowing this creep had likely been inside here while I was sleeping, the rain machine blocking out any sounds of footsteps or doors creaking open—it chilled me to the bone. Even with all the lights turned on, I still jumped at every shadow. I had Gabriel open the closet for me, and I couldn't put my feet near the bottom of the bed, even though I'd already checked to see that it was empty.

I just couldn't trust my own bedroom. My own house. I couldn't trust anything.

Except for Gabriel. He tried to help me pack but stepped aside after I nearly trampled over him running around my room. Of course, I needed to bring books, so I went to the bookshelf and grabbed a couple that were highest on my to-be-read list. I looked up at the hanging plant that dropped her green leaves down the soft brown wood of the bookshelf.

"Damn it, who's going to water my plants?"

"I can come back every now and then and give them some water," Gabriel said. He was leaning against the wall, arms crossed, looking like a mix between the Terminator and a teddy bear.

"So you're a bodyguard, a detective, and also a plant nanny?" I shook my head, a smile creeping on my face. "What else can you do?"

"I can cook a mean filet mignon."

"Great, a chef."

"And I can give some really great massages."

"Okay, bud, now you're just showing off. And also, I've been told *I'm* actually a great massager, so..." I chuckled as I lifted my suitcase so that it was on its wheels. "Honestly, I could use both of those things after the way tonight's gone."

"Well, the faster we get out of here, the faster you might get them."

I arched a brow, another chuckle rising from my chest. The fear still sat there, coiling beneath my ribs like a patient viper waiting to strike, but Gabriel's light teasing and bright blue gaze helped keep it at bay. "Are you bribing me to move faster?"

"Maybe."

"You said filet mignon and a massage, right?"

Gabriel nodded his head, lips tipping up into a smile that revealed a dimple. I grabbed the suitcase and broke out into a run, exaggerating my movements so that I was sure I looked like a cartoon character: flailing arms and legs as the suitcase rolled precariously alongside me.

I could hear Gabriel laughing all the way to the car. It was a sound I quickly found myself not only getting accustomed to but addicted to. I wanted to hear more of it. Even through the chaos and horror that tonight brought, I was able to find a light shining from the man by my side.

This is going to be interesting.

6

GABRIEL FERNANDEZ

TONIGHT HAD BEEN A WORST-CASE SCENARIO. My job was to keep people safe, and yet everyone's life was at risk. Thankfully, it was just some twisted mind games the Midnight Chemist decided to play, but next time, it might not just be old surveillance footage, and I had to be ready.

But first, I had to get Tristan out of his house and do it in a way that assured we weren't being followed. I made sure to take a winding route through the Atlanta suburbs on my way to the first Airbnb I had rented. It was a two-story home in a quiet and tree-lined community, everyone tucked away in their beds reading a book or watching TV. I parked the car and told Tristan to grab his bag.

"When we go in, just keep walking straight ahead. We're going to go through the yard and out onto the other side of the street. A car's waiting there to take us to where we're really staying."

Tristan cocked his head. I could tell there was fear and anxiety roiling up inside him, clear in his down-turned lips and furrowed brow. "How did you plan all this out so quick?"

"I'm not part of Stonewall Investigations *Elite* for nothing." I gave him a wink, and he returned it with a smile.

"Thank you, Gabriel. Seriously."

"Call me Gabe. And no thanks needed."

His smile grew, the wrinkles between his thick brows slowly disappearing. He had two tiny diamond stud earrings that glittered under the car lights. "Okay, Gabe, I take the thank-you back, then."

"Well, you don't have to do all that."

He laughed, a sound that filled the car and made my chest vibrate. I had to admit, Tristan was the kind of guy I'd hang out with even if I wasn't getting paid to do it. He had charm galore, humor that kept me in stitches, an interesting outlook on life, and looks that put a *GQ* cover model to shame.

Most of all, though, he was talented. I hadn't told him yet, but I read his books and was floored by how quickly they sucked me in and didn't let me go. I'd never been a big reader, besides a comic book–binging phase I went through in college. Books never called to me. I was always bothered by sitting down in one spot for too long. Audio-books had helped with that, but still, I hadn't found a story that really pulled me in.

Not until I read Tristan's work. From the first page, I was hooked. He had a way with words that wrapped me up. And his perspective as a gay Black man shone through the pages; even though the work was fiction, I could tell his life experiences had helped bring an authenticity to his characters that I hadn't found anywhere else.

"Ready?" he asked, a hand on the door handle, another holding the small suitcase between his legs.

"Let me go in first," I said.

He nodded, his smile flickering like a dying flame. It was the exact opposite of what I wanted to happen. I wanted to stoke that smile so that it burned from cheek to cheek, lighting the entire world on fire with its brilliance.

"Hey, Tristan—"

"You can call me Trist."

My turn to crack a smile. "Trist," I said, the name feeling familiar and new on my tongue. "You're going to be alright. I've got you. I'm not letting anything happen to you, okay? That fucker may have gotten close before, but I wasn't around for that. That is *not* happening again. I swear it."

He chewed on the inside of his cheek, his eyes looking for something in mine. I held his gaze, the space between us taking on a life of its own. Like invisible sparks suddenly ignited between us, popping against my nose, my face, my lips.

"I believe you," he said. "And I'm really grateful you're here."

"I am, too," I answered honestly as we got out of the car. I looked around the empty street, not seeing any suspicious cars or prying eyes. Crickets chirped from a bush on the pebbled path leading up to the front door, our shoes crunching over the rocks.

"What did you do before this? Before being a body-guard-detective hybrid?"

I tapped the password into the keypad before answering, wanting to get indoors as quickly as possible. "I was in the Marines. On my way to becoming an officer until I got a really bad knee injury. It took me out. I could barely walk for months. Still gets locked up every now and then."

"Damn, what happened?" Tristan asked as he rolled his suitcase through the silent home, decorated to be as basic and beige as possible.

"It's actually, well, uh, it's pretty embarrassing."

He cocked his head, lips slanting into a smirk. "I love embarrassing stories. I'll trade you one if you tell yours."

"Deal," I said, never having bargained for a life story before. "I was... getting ass shaking lessons and hit my knee against a chair, knocking it clean out of the socket. Had to get two surgeries to fix the damage."

Tristan paused just as we reached the back door, his jaw cracked open, his chin practically on the floor. I chuckled, not surprised at his reaction.

"I've had knee problems all my life, so it's not like ass shaking was the *sole* reason I had to be discharged from the Marines, but it played a big-ass part in it."

It was Tristan's turn to laugh. "I'm sorry, Gabe. I'm not laughing at your injury. I'm just trying to picture this brick wall of a man shaking his ass for the coin."

"I don't think you'd be laughing if you saw how good I've gotten at it."

He arched a brow and crossed his arms. I realized I had walked directly into a trap.

A thirst trap, to be exact. The most dangerous kind.

"Show me, then," he said, his smirk turning devilish.

I was about to say no. We had to keep going, had to get to the next Airbnb. But... it would make him smile. And that would be worth the minute or so of potential humiliation.

I turned, putting my hands up on the wall and arching my back a bit, pushing my ass out. I pressed my forehead against the wall and found myself smiling as I made my cheeks dance up and down, focusing on giving Tristan a damn show. His gasp told me all I needed to know as I kept going, using my hips to add a bit of swirl in there before I dropped down as far as my knees would let me.

Thankfully, I didn't need help getting back up. Now, *that* would be embarrassing.

I turned around to Tristan slow-clapping, that smile wide on his face. "That was impressive. I'm a little hypnotized if I'm being honest."

"I can get you even more hypnotized, but not because of my dance skills." I gave Tristan a wink, leaving his jaw cracked open again as he took in what I said. I didn't give him time to snap back, grabbing his suitcase and opening the door. "Come on, you can tell me your embarrassing story in the car."

"Ah shit, that's right. I forgot about that."

"I didn't," I said, rolling the suitcase out into the yard. I shut the door behind us and led us through the well-maintained yard. We went over to the fence, where a latched exit was lit by a nearby streetlamp. I opened the gate, and we stepped out onto the street that surrounded the property.

The black town car I ordered waited for us exactly where he said he'd be. A quick glance up and down the street told me no one was around. I opened the door for Tristan and got in after him, thanking the driver as I settled in.

"Wait until you see this next place," I said as we started to drive off.

"Better than this one?"

I gave him a guilty smile. "I splurged a little using the company card. Zane gave me the OK, though."

"Oh Lord," Tristan said, shaking his head. He fiddled with the silver chain around his neck, tucking it back under his black T-shirt. "Alright, so an embarrassing story... damn, I've got a few, actually. Hmm, let's go with the time I tripped and fell face-first into Ryan Reynolds' crotch."

I nearly choked on air. "That sounds less like an embarrassing moment and more like a wet dream."

"Oh, it was pretty much both. Except I wasn't dreaming. I was accepting an award for one of my books at the GLAAD Awards, and he was a presenter. He was onstage, standing by the podium, when I'm walking toward him and trip on *literally* nothing. I fall forward but in the weirdest way possible, right down on my knees.

The momentum pushes my face directly into Ryan's crotch. His instant reaction is to reach down and block me, but instead, his hands end up on the back of my head and lock me there for a few seconds, which felt like an entire eternity.

"Of course, the entire room broke out into raucous laughter and hoots. I made a joke about never washing my face again, which landed pretty well considering the moment."

I started to laugh sometime around the middle of his story, my stomach hurting as I pictured the scene.

"That is pretty embarrassing, but one hell of a story."

Tristan nodded, his smile still wide and his face lighting up. Even the driver was surprising some laughter. It was a very welcome contrast to the terror that had infiltrated earlier in the night. I wasn't letting my guard down by any means, but I did take a moment to relax into the seat, allowing myself to enjoy this moment, just like my therapist would have told me to.

"I've got pictures of it."

"No way, really?"

He looked out the window, giving me a moment to admire his side profile. I tried not to stare, but it was difficult when a man like Tristan was sitting only a couple of feet away from you. "We're trading again, though. One embarrassing photo for another."

I managed to flick my gaze away right before Tristan turned back to me. I didn't have many photos in my phone, but it looked like we were never meant to trade anyway since the driver slowed down at the front of a set of curling iron gates, blushing-red rosebushes lining up the tall brick wall that surrounded the property.

"Holy shit," Tristan said, leaning between the two front seats like an excited puppy. The gates opened, and the winding driveway led us up to our stay. "Are you fucking kidding me?"

"Nope," I said, seeing Tristan this excited making me irrationally happy. "Told you I splurged."

7

TRISTAN HALL

THIS WASN'T AN AIRBNB. It was an AirBnZ, encompassing the entire fucking alphabet.

"How did you even find this place? In the middle of Atlanta?"

"We aren't really in the middle," Gabe answered as we walked toward the castle made of sleek glass and modern lines. "Also, I did a shit ton of googling."

It looked like a house plucked right out of the Hollywood Hills, belonging to a famous film star who liked her homes extravagant and stylish. It was gray and white with black trim that made the extended porch appear like it was miles long, wrapping around the front of the home. The landscaping was equally as impressive, with emerald-green grass climbing up the slight incline that led to a bed of colorful peonies and tall sunflowers and pastel pink and blue orchids.

"Damn," I said as Gabriel opened the two towering frosted glass doors that led into the foyer. "I'm going to need to get stalked and threatened more often if it means staying in a place like this."

He chuckled as he shut the doors, clicking the heavy locks into place. "It's also got a state-of-the-art alarm system connected directly to the APD *and* the FBI. If the Midnight Chemist so much as steps a toe past those gates, they're done for."

"Does that mean some suited men and women are sitting in a dark room listening to us right now?"

"Possibly," Gabe said. "So watch what you say." He shot me a wink.

"Penis," I whispered.

He cocked his head. I wondered if he would catch on. Maybe he had never played this game? Maybe he didn't have an immature teenager controlling all of his more intrusive thoughts. I was about to explain when Gabriel repeated me, saying the word a little louder than my whisper.

"Penis," I echoed, saying it louder.

"Penis." Gabe spoke in his normal voice.

I raised mine. "Penis."

"Penis!"

"*Penis!*" I shouted at the top of my lungs before I bent over laughing, Gabe joining me.

Nothing to see here. Just two grown men laughing over a schoolyard game. I looked up, meeting Gabe's eyes, which glittered under the bright lights washing down from the vaulted ceiling. His strong brow and prominent jawline appeared to be etched out of stone, the shadows adding contrast that had to have been placed there by a master painter and charcoal. I had the sudden urge to run my thumb across those lines, tracing them until I reached his lips.

Shit. I caught myself staring. I blinked and looked away, rubbing the back of my neck. "There," I said. "At least our FBI agents know what we're about."

"Penis?"

"Obviously. Dick and cock, all day, every day."

Gabriel's smile slanted. Something simmered underneath those half-lidded eyes.

I had to go. The heat between us was rising, and I was scared I'd turn to ash. Or at least my brain would, and then I'd end up doing some dumb thing I'd regret once the morning came around.

I grabbed my bag and looked around the brightly lit and well-decorated foyer. "Alright, I'm going to shower and then try to figure out how the hell that surveillance video landed on my television screen like that."

"Want to meet in the living room? We can work together. I don't think I'm going to bed anytime soon."

I nodded, aware that my smile may be giving away how excited I was at the thought of spending more time with Gabe. "Sounds good to me." I tried to tamp it down, but my cheeks wouldn't listen, so I turned away instead, disappearing down a hallway I assumed would lead me to one of the bedrooms, finding it about fifteen minutes of wandering later.

———

MY MIND STARTED TO DRIFT. I'd been staring at this laptop screen for what felt like years. The text swam around the screen in little rivers of black against white, none of it making much sense. I felt like I was out of my league. I enjoyed tech, and I liked code—it felt like such a departure from the words I usually worked with while still being familiar—but I didn't have the skills I needed to figure out how that video got on my screen.

Which is where YouTube and wine came in. I clicked over to another educational video and leaned forward for my glass, taking a heavy chug as I pressed Play.

We were sat in the living room, surrounded by beautiful landscape paintings dotted with bright and surreal colors. The mirrored windows allowed us to see out toward the infinity edge pool and fire pit in the yard without any worry of someone being able to look in. Gabriel was on the other end of the couch from me, wearing a pair of black basketball shorts and a white tank top with Nike socks that went up past his ankle. He had one leg up on the couch and the other planted on the floor, his attention pinned to a file of police reports he collected on the most recent Midnight Chemist murders.

Damn. How the hell did that man manage to look that sexy while he flipped through pages of bloody crime scenes?

I took another (heavier) chug of the wine, nearly finishing my glass. I could feel that pre-buzz warmth settle into my bones. My shoulders relaxed, my toes wiggling against the plush white rug.

"How's it going?" I asked, pausing the video and

setting my laptop aside. "Because I'm starting to halluci-nate over here."

"Are you tired? You can go to bed, Trist. It's been a long-ass day."

I tried to ignore the tingle that spread through me at the sound of my nickname on Gabriel's lips. I glanced at my watch, seeing that it was only eleven. The day certainly had been long, but I wasn't ready to call it just yet. Not when Gabriel sat a couple of feet away from me looking the way he did, the shorts falling down the leg he had up on the couch, revealing quite a bit of muscular and hairy thigh—and a tattoo.

"Hold up," I said, leaning forward. "I didn't know you had tattoos."

"Just this one," Gabriel said. It was high up on his thigh. A black-and-white sketch of a hummingbird, its wings appearing to be in motion, its beak stretched up as if toward the sun. "Hummingbirds are my favorite animals. I'd get called out for it when I mentioned it. Something about a big guy like me liking something so delicate made people raise an eyebrow. It's dumb, but I hated it, so I decided to get one tattooed on me."

"It's not dumb at all," I said, admiring the intricate line work that made up the feathers. "I love it. You took something people tried to hold over you and made it yours. It's beautiful."

Gabriel smiled as he stretched out his leg, giving me a better view of not only the tattoo but also of his muscular thigh. The definition in his quads nearly made me drool.

"Thank you," he said. "I'm proud of it."

"Why hummingbirds?" I asked. I tried to get my mind back on track, but all I could think of was those damn turkey legs at Disney World. The ones that were the size of your head and you carried around for the majority of the day. Not that I wanted to bite into Gabe's thighs, but they still had the same mouthwatering effect.

"Because it's like they defy everything about the real world. In the way they fly, the way they hover, the way they eat, how incredibly fast their hearts beat. Plus, they're just these beautiful little comets of color shooting across a garden—what's not to love about them?"

Damn. And here I was thinking I was the wordsmith. "I've never really thought about it, but you're right. They are impossible little birds, aren't they?"

"Very. And I live for the impossible." His grin was an easy one to throw back. I didn't think I'd smiled this much in a while, definitely not since my whole ordeal started. And for all intents and purposes, after the shitshow that tonight had been, a smile should have been the hardest thing to muster.

But it wasn't. Not with Gabe around. Smiling was easy, forgetting about the world was easy. Everything felt *easy*, even though there was someone out there who wanted me dead. How did that work? What kind of magic was Gabriel working on me?

"How about yours?" Gabriel asked, leaning in to look at the tattoo on my forearm. It was a black-and-white line-drawn image of two palm trees side by side.

"I found out I got my first book deal when we were on vacation in Miami Beach, so I got these two palm trees to commemorate it. The leaves touching there look like an *M* for 'Miami' but also for the title of my first book: *Mad Love*."

"It's beautiful," Gabriel said, doing something that surprised the fuck out of me.

He traced it. With his finger. Only briefly, but enough to make me swallow a massive lump of... something. Nerves? Lust?

"So," I said, clearing my throat, my thoughts steering back to the issue at hand, "what have you figured out? Anything yet?" I glanced over at Gabe's lap, where the case files sat.

He looked down to the files, acting as if I had snapped him out of something. "Yeah, actually. I'm honing in on the chemical this person is using to make his kills. It's rare, and it's not something you can just order off of Amazon."

"What is it?" I asked, perking up and leaning over to get a closer look at the files.

"It's a type of poison found only in sea anemones. One particular sea anemone, to be exact: Rhodactis howesii. It's so toxic that just eating it uncooked will send the person into a paralytic shock, where they later die from pulmonary edema." I gave him a blank look. "They drown in their own fluids."

I winced. That part I understood. "Shit... a sea anemone? What the fuck?"

"It's not the only toxin they use, but it's the primary one."

"Okay, well, that's a good thing, right? There can't be tons of Red-dicktus Hawaiis around, right?"

Gabe arched a brow before laughter bubbled up his chest. "I'm narrowing down a few suppliers of these Red-dicktus Hawaiis," he said with a wink.

"Alright, listen here, buddy. I might be a best-selling author, but I don't have a zoology degree. I don't know how to pronounce that shit." I smirked and elbowed Gabe's side. I could handle jokes and often made fun of myself before anyone else, but getting ribbed by Gabriel felt different. Not in a bad way, either.

Hold up... how'd we get so close? I could feel his breath on my cheek. I could almost feel the body heat radiating off those firm muscles. I licked my lips, suddenly aware of the rapidly quickening beat of my heart. My chest filled with a flushed sensation as blood went everywhere but my brain, my thoughts becoming hazy with something I could only describe as lust.

His eyes. They were on mine, searching through mine. For what, I had no idea. But I allowed it, looking back into those deep pools of ocean blue twinkling with light that rivaled that of the stars. Handsome didn't even touch half of what this man was. Adonis? Greek god? Perfection?

The space between us disappeared. I wasn't sure who made the first move, me or him or both. All I knew was that the earth quaked when our lips met for the first time. A tremor that extended up through the floor, through my feet, up my spine, shaking my entire being.

I parted his lips with mine, my tongue slipping in,

finding his. He gripped the nape of my neck, his fingers applying a pressure that almost unwound me right then and there. I moved closer to him, pushing him up against the arm of the couch as our kiss deepened, the tidal wave of our chemistry cresting over the horizon, its monstrous size ready to devour us.

A thought struck me and froze me in place, like a bucket of ice being dropped over my head.

Gabriel opened his eyes, stopping the kiss. "What? What's wrong?"

"This isn't against the rules, right? Are there rules about hooking up with your bodyguard?"

Gabriel's smirk was glistening. "It isn't exactly encouraged, but there's nothing explicitly said about it."

"Okay, great, keep kissing me, then."

He licked his lips, his cocky smile nearly knocking me to my knees. "Gladly." He grabbed my head in his hands and locked his lips with mine. Heat bloomed inside my core like a rosebud on fire, its petals singed with flame. Gabe must have felt the same passion because his kiss became more aggressive, more hungry. He pushed a leg underneath me and grabbed my hip, pulling me onto his lap, pushing his hips up so that he was sure I felt how turned on he was.

The rest of the world disappeared out from under me. Nothing else mattered. Nothing but Gabriel's lips on my throat, his tongue against my skin, his hands under my shirt, his hard cock against my ass.

Nothing else mattered but us.

8

GABRIEL FERNANDEZ

MY ENTIRE BODY felt like a live wire whipping in hurricane-force winds, sparking and exploding as if each cell in my body contained a bundle of lit fireworks. My hands roamed his body, feeling his soft skin under his shirt, running up over his chest, his pebbled nipples pressed against my palms. I squeezed, earning a moan from Tristan, one which I immediately swallowed.

His kiss was everything I'd never had. Passion and lust and heat and life. I'd had boyfriends in the past; I'd had hookups, one-night stands, and fiery summer flings.

None of them compared to the chemical explosion that came from Tristan's lips on mine. Enough to power an entire nuclear reactor. And I wanted more.

Immediately, a crimson-red hunger consumed me. I grabbed at the bottom of his shirt, rocking my hips up so that he could feel how hard this made me. I wasn't shy about it. I wanted him to know the lust he lit inside my core, and judging by the intensifying moans slipping from his lips, I was doing just that.

And judging by the stiffness rubbing against my stomach, he was feeling the exact same.

"Fuck," I said against his lips, my hands sliding under his shirt and over his silky soft skin. "You're a really good kisser."

"So are you, sir."

"Mmm," I said, a low growl forming at the base of my throat. "I like it when you call me that."

"Oh, really?" Tristan reached down between us and grabbed a handful of my cock. "Sir."

I dropped my head back with a sigh and throbbed in his grip. "Gah damn, how do you already have me so close?"

Tristan simply smiled that thousand-watt smile of his and pushed my shorts up my thigh, reaching inside and pulling out my hard cock, the tip already glistening with precome. Tristan licked his lips, the smile going nowhere as he slowly dropped down to the floor, both hands on my knees as he pushed my legs open wider, my cock pulsing outside of my shorts.

"Wow," he said, grabbing me with both hands. His honey-brown eyes filled with something close to admiration. "You're huge."

I chuckled and looked down at the massive bulge between Tristan's legs. "Looks like I'm not the only one, either. Go on. Show me."

Tristan cocked his head, his grin turning devilish as he stood up, dropping his shorts and briefs, exposing the most delicious-looking dick I'd ever seen in my entire fucking life. He was long, thick, uncircumcised, with a perfect set of full balls that had my mouth watering. His pubes were trimmed and dark against his skin, "Fuck, get over here. I have to taste you."

"Yes, sir," Tristan said, the word falling from his lips and shooting straight to my core, precome oozing from my twitching cock. "But you have to lay down. I want to taste you, too."

I lay down on the couch, spreading my legs and holding my cock up with a thumb at the base, watching as Tristan came toward me, his own hard dick swinging in the air. He was beautiful. A perfect specimen of a man, and I was the lucky one who got to play around with him. How the hell had that happened?

He gracefully climbed onto the couch, one knee on either side of me, his juicy bubble butt now in my face. "Hold on," I said before he leaned forward to take me in his mouth. I grabbed his hips and pulled him back, burying my face in his ass. He gasped, his body tensing a moment before I felt him relax. I started to kiss him, each cheek, nipping at his skin, breathing him in. He smelled like fresh laundry and warm sex, like a glass of top-shelf whiskey. I wanted to drink him in. I opened his cheeks and tongued his crack, earning the loudest moan yet. My cock throbbed as his hands closed around my shaft.

Tristan sat on my face as he spit in his hand and started to jerk me off. Heaven didn't even describe it. This was beyond a fantasy. I let myself get lost in the moment, enjoying every sensation, every swirl of my tongue, every twist of his hand. I stretched my legs, curling my toes against a soft pillow, kicking it down to the floor as Tristan's wet, hot mouth closed around my cock. The warm leather of the couch stuck to my ass, mixing with the sweat that started to bead across my body.

I groaned into Tristan's hole, his entire body shivering against me. He lifted up and shifted, legs on either side of my face now as the head of his cock brushed against my lips, painting me with his salty-sweet taste. I licked his leaking slit before grabbing him and opening my mouth for him.

His taste exploded all over my tongue as I blew him. The room filled with the gurgling wet sounds of dick-sucking. My favorite kind of ASMR. Tristan's balls were on my nose as I tried to deep-throat him, his cock hitting the back of my throat with a gag. He started to thrust downward, fucking my mouth. I followed suit, rutting my hips up, burying my cock in his mouth. Pleasure rocked over me like a tidal wave, pulling me off into the deep end. I closed my eyes and sucked, my core tightening as my climax raced toward me like an out-of-control bullet train.

I took Tristan's dick out of my mouth, sucking in a deep breath of air before warning him. "I'm close, baby."

Tristan leaned up, his cock head pressing against my cheek as I looked down, my rock-hard dick glistening in his hands. I could feel the pressure building inside me, coiling like a snake around my gut. I went back to sucking Tristan's cock, unable to get enough of him down my throat to satiate the hunger I had for him. All-consuming. I loved every drop I could taste of him, the way he smelled, the way he writhed above me as he wrapped his tongue around the head of my dick.

Tristan rose up, dick still in my mouth, and gave a grunt-shout hybrid as he unloaded into my mouth. I managed to swallow most of it, taking it down like a shot, hungry for more, riding the wave that had almost knocked Tristan to his knees.

My climax hit with the same exact force, ropes of come shooting from my cock. Lightning crashed through my body, tendrils of electricity branching out through every muscle and bone. Pure fucking ecstasy. I dropped my head back and managed to suck some air into my breathless lungs. The view I had of Tristan's ass and balls made me wish I was a painter. I figured I could make a killing selling erotic nudes of such a masterpiece.

He slowly turned his body so that we were face-to-face, cock-to-cock, both of us still swollen and sticky. His smile matched the force of sunshine I felt lighting up the inside of my chest. What the hell had just happened? Was that a hookup, or did we just fuck ourselves into a goddamn storybook?

"That was really fucking hot... sir." Tristan shot me a wink and leaned in for a long and wet kiss. I could feel him getting hard again, his cock pushing against mine for space. I opened my legs so he fit perfectly between them. Something about his weight on me felt comforting. Like I was home, even though this place was nothing like home.

For a long time, I wasn't even sure where home was.

"If I knew I'd be getting this kind of service from my hot bodyguard-detective hybrid, then I would have tried attracting the attention of a serial killer way sooner."

Tristan's dark humor got a surprised laugh out of me. It was good to hear him joke about it. I always felt like taking an otherwise fucked-up situation and turning it on its head with a joke was a good way toward moving past it.

"I'd prefer we met a different way, but I guess this was what fate had in store." I had a lazy hand on Tristan's hip, making soft, slow circles with my thumb.

"And you promise this won't fuck anything up, right? Like you aren't going to get fired or anything for hooking up with me?"

I shook my head. "No, I won't get fired. I might get a reprimand, but only because distractions are easier to come upon when you're watching over someone like you."

His golden eyes glittered, matching the brightness of his smile. The living room lights were on, bathing the oversized space in a soft white glow. "I think we can keep getting a little distracted tonight. We can worry about my case tomorrow."

He gave his hips a little wiggle, rubbing himself on me, a string of come wetting my stomach.

"Do you have any plans for tomorrow?" he asked, wiggling again, his casual smile at odds with the devastating inferno he was lighting in my core.

"I do," I said, a growl slipping into my words. I reached around and rubbed his ass, pulling him down onto me. "I want to go to the APD and see if they have anything else they can give me. I think Eric's going with me."

"Good, I'm joining."

"Huh?"

"I shouldn't really be left alone, anyways." He leaned down, his tongue flicking against my upper lip. "Think we'll find something?"

"I hope so," I said, my thoughts disintegrating faster than tissue paper in a cup of water. "I think Eric says he knows someone there. I'm hoping they have something they're holding on to."

"Why wouldn't they just work with you to begin with?"

I shrugged, stealing a kiss from Tristan. "Information is power. If something leaks about the serial killer and makes it onto the evening news, then that person now knows what to change and what to switch up so that we lose their trail. I get it. I don't like it, but I get it."

Tristan's wiggle turned into a thrust this time. "Alright," he said, his voice dropping low. "Let's worry about that tomorrow. Tonight, we hook up on every surface of this mansion as if it were ours."

And we did exactly that.

————

THE COPS HAD nothing for us. We left the station empty-handed. Eric had joined us early that morning. We grabbed some coffee and went to meet with the sheriff, who had a working relationship with Eric. She assured us that I already had all the information they did. At first, I wanted to push, but I could tell Eric trusted her, and I didn't want to be the one to strain their relationship, so I thanked her for her time and left with Eric and Tristan.

We stepped out into a bright and warm summer day, a handful of cotton-candy clouds drifting across the bright blue sky. I could see the disappointment in Tristan's eyes. Such a contrast to the blissed-out ecstasy that had been reflected in them only hours before.

We had talked about things over breakfast, deciding to keep whatever was happening between just the two of us for now. Neither of us was quite sure what was happening or where this was headed, but we *were* sure that we wanted to see it play out. And that meant protecting the flame for now, shielding it from outside forces. I liked that. It felt like the two of us had a secret, tucked away from prying eyes.

"Well, that was a waste of time," Tristan said. Eric reached out and gave him a supportive shoulder squeeze.

"It wasn't the end-all, be-all. I'm sure Gabriel will be able to put the pieces together. I've got more trust in him than the cops, anyway."

Tristan nodded, although I could still sense the disappointment. It made me want to reach out and hug him. Hold him. Tell him that I was going to work day and night to make sure this psycho fucker was locked up.

"I've got this," I said instead, trying to give all those emotions with a simple look. Tristan's smile wavered, flickered. It lit, catching the spark and pushing up at his cheeks.

Eric raised his phone, looking over his sunglasses. "Colt just text me. He said he and some of the group is getting together to ride scooters down the Beltline. Wanna join?"

Tristan looked to me. I wanted to continue working on the case, figuring I should track down some people for a couple of interviews, but I saw how badly Tristan needed this time.

"Let's do it," I said. Tristan's smile blossomed like the trees exploding with life after a rough winter.

Similar to how my heart had been feeling these last few days. Like the thaw of an icy-cold stretch of years was beginning to take hold, warmth pumping back into my chest, mixed with feelings I hadn't experienced in a long while: giddy and playful and hopeful and so fucking thrown off my orbit.

Just don't get distracted. It'll be fine.

My eyes dropped down to Tristan's ass, looking like a full meal in his khaki shorts. An entire bus full of serial killers could have driven past with a banner advertising their murders, and I would have missed it.

9

TRISTAN HALL

HE HAD EYES LIKE AN OCEAN, and all I wanted to do was swim in them.

Yes, yes, I know that's a stereotypical phrase for any wordsy author to use, but what do you expect from someone who makes a living off swoony words tinted in purple prose? It's how I operated, how I moved through the world, and even with my spark struggling to light under all the stress, Gabriel still made those words flow.

In fact, I had woken up two hours earlier than usual today and managed to write an entire chapter in my work in progress. I hadn't been able to get down those many consecutive words without interruption in months, maybe years.

And they were good words, too. I was confident about every letter I typed, every sentence I formed. It was a groove I slipped into and rode all the way until the sun came up and Gabriel padded out of the bedroom, rubbing his eyes as he walked toward the dining room table, where I had posted up.

Also where we proceeded to eat each other up for breakfast. Could you really blame me? When a half-naked man with a practically see-through pair of white shorts is walking toward you, his morning wood swinging left to right, it's only good manners to take care of it.

Now we were riding scooters down a crowded Belt-line, a row of brightly painted boutique shops on our right. A pet store, a CBD store, a small cafe, all with big and bold art painted across their facades. My friends were with us—Eric, Colton, Noah, and Jake. Yvette and her new boyfriend joined us, while the others were going to meet us for lunch.

These last twenty-four hours were exactly what I needed. There was still quite a bit left to unpack after last night, but already I could tell my soul was no longer running on empty. Even after the disappointing trip to the police department. Even after the targeted message I had received on my own damn television screen. I looked up at the sunny sky as the wind brushed past me, Gabriel at my side, looking a little comical with his large frame slightly hunched on the bright green electric scooter.

"Having fun?" I asked, flashes of last night (and this morning) going through my head.

Heat. Sweat. Come. Hard muscles. Lips on lips, cock on cock.

"I am," he answered with a smile I wanted to lick right off. "You?"

"Me too." I pushed down on the accelerator handle

and boosted forward, the scooter automatically sticking to the speed limit set on the pedestrian pathway. We were headed to Ponce City Market, an industrial red-bricked building that had been converted into a multitude of mouthwatering food spots and local stores, with residential lofts and apartments sitting just underneath a rooftop hangout spot equipped with everything from a bar to a mini-golf course.

"Hey, man," Colton said, matching my speed as we zipped past a bustling brewery, the sounds of a live band leaking over the black wooden fence. "How are you doing after yesterday?"

"I'm doing alright. Grateful I don't have to stay at my house, though. I can't believe that monster was in there."

Colton shook his head, his face bleaching with the same fear I felt gnaw at my ribs. "It's so fucked-up. But you've got us, and you've got Gabriel. It's going to be okay. In fact, Eric and I are going to lock ourselves inside the house and spend all weekend researching serial killers. I feel like all I know about them is shit from the movies, but maybe if we're able to get inside this person's head, then we can figure out their next move and catch them."

"You guys really don't have to do that." My heart swelled with warmth for my friends. This group had been through a ton of shit together; I didn't want to put them through any more. "Seriously, I don't want anyone else getting involved. Having you all at my house when that video came on was bad enough."

"Tristan, you helped me figure out who was behind

my mom's death. I owe you." Colton's light brown hair caught the sun and spun it like golden threads shining through. He had a kind face, one that looked even kinder now that he was extending such a gracious gift: his help.

"Thanks, Colt." It was all I could say before I started to feel choked up. Eric was a lucky guy to reunite with Colton. Their lives could have easily splintered off into a thousand different directions, never crossing again. But here they were, fresh off a honeymoon trip to Disney World, eyes full of love for each other.

It made me happy for my best friend and also wishful for myself. I tried to imagine the same happy ending for me, but all I could see ahead was a fog of heavy gray blotting out the horizon of my life. I had no idea if I was even going to be around in a few months, as morbid a thought as that was, but unfortunately, it was a reality I had to face when I had a bright red bullseye painted across my chest.

Thankfully, I didn't have much time to simmer on that thought. We crossed over a concrete bridge and pulled up to a row of parked scooters right outside the entrance to the market. Jess, Tia, and Steven were already waiting for us at the steps, Steven sucking on a bright yellow Popsicle.

"The gang's all here," Jess said as hugs were exchanged. She matched with Tia, wearing a blue T-shirt with black shorts. "We didn't plan this," she was quick to point out.

"Happens to us all the time," Noah said with a wave of his hand. Today was one of those times: both Noah and Jake wore green shirts, although Noah wore khaki shorts, and Jake wore black. "Guys ready to go eat?"

"Let's go," Eddy said, rubbing his stomach before putting a hand across Yvette's shoulders. He seemed to be warming up to us. I was surprised he hadn't been scared off after yesterday's debacle.

We walked through a covered area full of tables and chairs; someone playing the piano at the very end of the walkway added a lively soundtrack. "What's everyone in the mood for?" I asked the group.

"I can do Cuban," Noah said.

"Same," Jake and Jess both piped in.

"I'll probably grab something at that chicken spot," Eric said. I was about to tell him I'd join when my phone buzzed in the pocket of my jeans. I pulled it out, expecting some text about a late bill or an email about a forgotten deadline, but instead, what I received was something plucked directly out of my worst nightmare.

It was an unknown number, but the text told me all I needed to know about who was contacting me.

I hadn't realized I'd stopped walking. Gabriel was saying something, but I couldn't hear over the pounding of blood that echoed in between my ears. My hand started to shake. Gabriel took the phone from me as I stumbled backward, moving to one of the open benches and slumping down as soon as my knees gave way.

Gabriel read the message and immediately went into defense mode, his eyes raking through the crowd. I watched the twitch in his jaw, the tightening fist around my phone. But I knew he wouldn't spot him. Even though the Midnight Chemist clearly knew where I was.

The message had read: *Tristan, you have become my obsession beyond obsessions. I want to keep you in a tank, watching you float. Instead, I'll settle for watching you spend quality time with your friends. Enjoy Ponce. Order something good for me.*

We were surrounded by people, and now all of them felt like suspects. I looked to the couple walking down the path, hand in hand, the girl smiling and the guy mean-mugging me. A group of guys behind them caught my attention next, one of them looking like a Jeffrey Dahmer cosplayer. His beady black eyes were trained directly on me. To his left, a woman wearing a hat low on her head stared at me.

Two men, walking straight toward me.

A woman wearing a dark red shirt that looked to be soaked in blood was being pulled in my direction by the massive Rottweiler on a flimsy leash.

Panic started to rise like bile in my chest, bubbling up toward my mouth. I had never felt this kind of raw fear before. I squeezed my hands together as Eric and Yvette came to sit on either side of me. Noah, Jake, Steven, and Tia fanned out through the crowd, looking for anyone suspicious that might be lurking in the swarm of anony-mous faces.

This was all my fault. I had brought this attention into my life, and now I was dragging my friends directly into the eye of the storm. If anything happened to any of them...

"We have to go," Gabriel said, a firm hand on my shoulder. His tone snapped me out of my spiraling thoughts. I looked up to see his sturdy frame look shaken. This was the second time in as many days that the Midnight Chemist got past him, and that fact was enough to scare us both.

He was much better at holding it together than I was. I could barely stand. Part of me wanted to run until the horizon dropped from underneath me, and the other part wanted to stay right where I was until this sick fucker was lured out into the open. End it once and for all.

I didn't do either of those things. "I'm taking us back," Gabriel said, speaking to me but his gaze turned to the crowd. "Everyone needs to split up and take a long way home."

"I'm going with you guys." It was Eric. Colton was by his side, nodding.

"Us too," Jake said, his hand holding tight to Noah's. "We aren't leaving you alone, Tristan. We're going to help figure this out."

Jess and Tia came up right as the tears started to flow. I dabbed at my cheeks and got them under control before I started bawling as the piano performer crescendoed in her song. They agreed—they wanted to stick together.

But when Yvette said she was doing the same, Eddy turned into a clammy mess. He clearly was freaked-out by what was happening, and I couldn't blame him. He wanted to be as far from the situation as possible. It would likely be the smartest thing for any of them to do.

"If you need anything, please call me," she said as she

hugged me tight, her curls tickling the side of my face, the coconut scent of her lotion filling my nose. She left with Eric and Steven on either side of her, disappearing down the walkway. I tried not to imagine someone breaking off from the cluster of strangers, following them all the way to their cars, chasing them quietly until they made it to their apartments, where he'd slither in through a cracked open window and—

"Come," Gabriel said, his hand on my elbow. His grip was firm, but his eyes were soft, compassionate. This brick wall of a man was clearly affected by this. It made me scared, but it also made me realize how invested Gabriel was. Maybe too invested? Maybe this would cause blind spots, would create openings?

Doubt crept into my chest and nestled up next to the panic, creating a twisted little den of dark emotions. I tried not to let it grow, keeping it contained to a small piece of me. This situation was the darkest shit to have ever happened to me, but I had to somehow keep a positive outlook, or I'd be pulled under.

I looked into Gabriel's eyes. Sunlight slashed into them. Blue and dark, just like the ocean. I thought of how easy it'd be to drown in them.

10

GABRIEL FERNANDEZ

THIS WAS the reason why we shouldn't get close to our clients. Why I never should have allowed emotions to enter this equation. I should have kept the brick wall up.

I'd made a mistake. I wanted to see Tristan happy, wanted to see him smile. When they suggested going out for a walk and some lunch, red flags immediately shot up. I should have Tristan locked up in a room where only I could get to him, not traipsing around Atlanta with his friends, not when he was actively being hunted by a sadistic serial killer.

Instead, I let it happen. I went along for the ride, distracted by Tristan's wide smile and carefree laugh. He had seemed the calmest he'd been since I arrived. It felt like a gift, one he gave me with every twinkle of his golden gaze.

That gaze was no longer twinkling. It was turned down to the floor, Tristan's head in his hands. We were back in the Airbnb, the group gathered in the bougie living room, fear reflected on all their faces. Noah and Jake were on the couch, flicking through the crime reports I had acquired from the police, while Eric sat next to Tristan, a friendly hand on his shoulder.

Colton came down the hallway with a few bottles of water. He handed them out and sat next to Eric, eyes wide, as if he'd seen a ghost in the kitchen.

I cracked my knuckles and looked back down at my laptop. I had managed to get the surveillance footage from a few shops that were around us at the time of the text, but scrubbing through them was giving me nothing except a headache. Face and bodies swirled together as I sped up the tape, slowing it down, speeding it up. I'd look to see if there was anyone with a phone in their hands at the time the text was sent, which was actually quite a few people. And none of them seemed to be paying any attention to Tristan, who was just off frame in the one video I currently watched.

"What about calling the phone company?" Tia asked. She was sat at the small glass table next to one of the arching windows, the creamy white blinds drawn shut. "Can they tell us who sent the text?"

"I've already put in a request," I said. "But I doubt they'll get anything useful. Every text Tristan's gotten has come from an untraceable burner phone."

"Still, maybe we can at least get a location?" Jess suggested.

Tristan shook his head and sat back on the couch, rubbing his face. "We know the location. He was right next to us." I could hear the pain constricting Tristan's voice. I understood that fear. I felt it when I had fought alongside my friends, life-or-death decisions made on the fly as we jumped off our barges and infiltrated a run-down hideout, where bullets flew and lives were taken. I'd felt the same kind of fear that spread through Tristan like poison.

And I hated it. Hated that this had to be his path.

"Jess is right," I said, wanting to inject a little hope into the situation. "Any information we get at this point is useful. Knowing where that text was sent from could help us narrow things down. Maybe they weren't as close to us as we think."

Noah perked up, nudging his glasses up his nose. He cleared his throat. "Could there be some kind of tracker on you?"

I cocked my head at that. Tristan shrugged, patting his chest and legs. "Nothing that I'm aware of."

"Noah, maybe you're onto something. Tristan, where's your wallet?"

"My wallet? It's over there on the counter."

I set my laptop down on the blue-and-white rug and walked to the counter, grabbing the thin black wallet underneath a set of house keys. I opened it and looked through the different sections, taking out the cards and cash and setting them on the marble counter.

Nothing. It was worth a shot.

I started to place everything back when a card caught my attention. The expiration date was set for 2089... "Hey, Tristan, is this a mistake?" I lifted the slightly heavy red card.

Tristan tilted his head and squinted in my direction. He chewed on the inside of his cheek. "I don't recognize that card. Hold on." He stood from the couch, grabbing the card from my hand. He turned it over, shaking his head. "No, I never opened this card. I don't know..."

"Give it to me," I said. He handed the card back. I went directly into the kitchen and grabbed scissors from the butcher block. I cut the card, the two pieces falling onto the floor.

A wire was hanging from one of the pieces. A wire that should never have been inside of a credit card.

"Holy shit," Tristan said. He had followed me into the kitchen. He crouched and picked up the pieces of plastic. "This was how he's been tracking me?"

"He must have placed it in there that night he broke into your house."

Tristan dropped the card and leaned back on the kitchen island, his arms clutching tight around his chest. "So he knows we're here? Shit."

"We'll have to move again tonight," I said. I reached across what felt like miles, my hand closing around Tristan's. I held his gaze locked with mine, our hands over his chest, his heartbeat fluttering like a caged hummingbird. "I'm so sorry this is happening, Trist. But I'm going to get us through to the other side."

He sucked in a breath. It had a rattle to it, like he was holding back tears.

This next part would hurt the worst, but it was needed. "And I think we should put things on pause between us, at least until I do."

Tristan blinked a couple of times. His upper lift quaked momentarily before going stone stiff. The ice machine in the refrigerator whirled and roared.

I felt the need to elaborate. To explain that I wasn't putting a stop to anything, just a pause. Just to keep my head clear.

He cut me off. "I get it," he said, stepping back so that my hand fell from his. "And I think it's the smart thing to do. You probably shouldn't be getting attached to someone you're likely to lose, anyway."

"Tristan, that isn't what I meant. I'm upset with myself for making stupid mistakes. I can't have my head clouded with thoughts of kissing you while I'm charged with protecting you."

He rubbed at the sides of his head. "I know, you're right. I'm just—it's a lot of stress. I'm sorry."

"Don't ever apologize for any of this." I pointed toward the open archway leading out toward the living room, through a hall filled with potted plants. "Let's go back to the group and let them know what we found."

"Damn it, I hate how they're putting themselves in danger because of me."

"They're just trying to help. They care about you."

Tristan pushed off the island and turned away from me right as a glitter of a tear slid down his cheek. He walked away from me, shoulders slumped, the weight of his situation pushing down on him harder than gravity. I followed behind him, walking past a row of lush green ferns set inside cracked stone pots.

All eyes turned to us when we reentered the living room.

"We've got to go," Tristan said. He raised the cut pieces of the card. "The fucker's been tracking me."

"Jesus," Noah whispered. Jess dropped her face into her hands. Colton hissed. Eric got up and went for the card.

"So this is how he knew where you were," Eric said. He looked at the broken pieces of the card as if they held all the answers.

Tristan nodded. "I feel so fucking... invaded. This person has basically been watching me this entire time. Who knows if they could even hear me through there."

It was an unsettling thought. Pinpricks formed at the base of my neck, like someone had their eyes pinned to my back. I knew it was nothing, but I still glanced over my shoulder at the empty hallway we had just walked through.

Nothing. No one.

"Where are you guys going to go?" Jake asked.

"I'd rather not say that out loud," I said.

"Right, duh." Jake bit his nails. Anxiety was clear on all their faces. Tia looked like she was ready to bolt, keys already in hand and nervous looks thrown toward the front door. It was my cue. I had to get Tristan to safety and let everyone else find comfort in their homes, where they'd no doubt lock their doors and windows with extra care tonight.

I stepped forward, looking at the gathered group of fearful friends. "Alright, I want us to leave here in a staggered pattern. Jake and Noah will go first, then Tia and Jess, then Eric and Colton. Take the long routes home, and always keep an eye on your rearview. If you even have a *thought* that you're being followed, then stop where you're going and stay at the nearest hotel."

The group stood, the silence in the room only working to heighten the anxiety. No one quite knew what to say. No one really understood how to handle this. A serial killer stalking one of their own. How could anyone cope with that kind of reality?

Tristan and I were the last to leave. I looked back at the massive glass-and-stone mansion that had served as our brief hideout, tall green trees highlighted by moonlight smothering it. The drive was silent. Tristan didn't even ask where we were going, only speaking when I pulled into the brick driveway.

"Where are we?" he asked, looking out at the modest one-floor farmhouse.

"Home," I said, hitting a button on my car's dash and opening the garage door.

11

TRISTAN HALL

"HOME," Gabriel said as the garage door loudly rose to reveal a very well-organized space big enough to fit one car and a few bikes. I'd been so lost in my thoughts I hadn't really focused on *where* Gabriel had been taking us, so I was slightly surprised to see that we were at his house.

"I didn't realize you had a house in Atlanta. I thought you were from New York?"

He shook his head as he pulled into his parking spot. "I lived there for a few years—it's how I started working with Stonewall Investigations—but I've always had a home base here in Atlanta. It's one of the reasons Zane assigned me to your case. I was born and raised in Marietta."

"Huh," I said, looking around at the quiet neighborhood. It was a street full of flipped homes with clean white exteriors and bold-colored trims. Porches that were well maintained and fences that needed no repairs. It was silent except for the low din of a TV coming from an open window.

"Come, let's get inside. I've got a nice bottle of wine waiting for us."

"What's the occasion?" I asked and followed him to the front door.

"Life being shit is the occasion."

I chuckled at that. Gabriel unlocked his front door and stepped inside, tapping a series of numbers into the beeping alarm.

Instantly, the sweet scent of fresh flowers bloomed all around me. I noticed he had a couple of diffusers and a Glade plug-in close to the door. He kicked off his sneakers and placed them on a neatly organized shoe rack. I followed suit, rolling in my suitcase and setting it to the side. Gabriel shut and locked the door and set the alarm back on.

"Your place is beautiful," I said, taking it in for the first time. A mixture of modern decor and some slightly more dated touches. There was a trendy brown leather couch on a fluffy white rug that felt like a puffy cloud under my toes. The entertainment center was a scratched-up brown unit that could have used a little upgrade, but I didn't blame him for spending that money on the massive TV that took up most of the wall, a sound system flanking it and turning the living room into an immersive theatre. A couple of paintings hung on the wall, a mixture of what appeared to be oil and watercolor, creating an interesting dynamic that made the landscapes appear as if they were shifting whenever I moved.

"And these are just stunning," I said, admiring the painting closest to me.

"Thank you," he said, stepping beside me. I could almost feel an electrical current zapping off his forearm, tickling at mine.

But no. We need to keep things cool between us.

"I painted these a few years ago."

My jaw dropped, and my head turned to him as if on a swivel. "You made these?"

"You don't have to look so surprised," Gabriel said, bushy brow arched and a smile half-cocked on his face. "You're not the only creative one here."

I stammered, realizing how rude I'd just sounded. "That's not, no, I just mean—"

"I'm teasing you. I know it's a little surprising. A brush in my hand probably looks like an elephant holding a stick."

"A silverback, actually." Tristan shot me a wink.

"How did you know I was graying back there?" I gave an exaggerated crane of my neck as if I were checking under my shirt. He started to laugh, giving me that sound I was getting so fucking attached to.

"Well, these are beautiful. Really, Gabe. The way you play with different mediums and make it all flow together is insane to me."

"Same as the way you put together all those different words and make it a coherent story. Now, *that's* insane." He cocked his head, eyes searching mine. For what, I wasn't sure, but I allowed it. "Have you been working on anything recently?"

Ah, there it was. The question that I'd grown to hate over the last couple of months. I used to be able to answer that with an enthusiastic yes, launching into quick elevator pitches of whatever books I had been writing at the time. The passion would ooze out of me, the words flowing like a babbling brook, unable to keep quiet for long. My muse had always worked overtime, causing me to frequently pause conversations and jot something down in my Notes app as a new story element developed out of thin air.

Not anymore. Stress and worry had caused my well of words to dry up. I sat at my computer and stared at a blank screen, feeling nothing but a sad emptiness. Everything I wrote down felt fake and fabricated, as if I were painting by the numbers and not with my heart.

Until a few days ago, at least. After Gabe and I got together, I remember waking up feeling as if I could write a saga elaborate enough to take on *Dante's Inferno*. I had managed to get a good amount of (good) words down on my work in progress, with random ideas popping up throughout the day. "I am," I said. "It's been difficult keeping focus with everything going on, but I think my muse is finally coming back."

And I've got you to thank for that.

"Good, because the world needs more of your books. Trust me."

I narrowed my eyes at him. That sounded a whole lot like he had read my work. I crossed my arms, my eyelids turning to slits. "You haven't read my stuff, have you?"

His shit-eating grin told me all I needed to know. I

gave him a half-hearted punch to the chest. "Asshole. I told you when we met not to read my books. I get too in my head... did you like it?"

"Like it? I loved it. And I'm not a huge reader, so that's a huge compliment."

That got a genuine smile out of me. It was a refreshing reminder and made me want to sit down and get some more words out. I had my laptop with me, so maybe that would be a possibility. I went for my suitcase and looked around the cozy space, oddly feeling at home, even though it had been the first time I had stepped into this place.

"Where can I drop my stuff off?"

"Right over here," he said, guiding me down a short hallway and into a guest bedroom, plush white sheets perfectly made and crowned with a wall of blue and beige pillows. There was a dresser with an ancient-looking television perched on top of it, a window next to it that looked out into his sizable yard.

I closed the blinds. I didn't like looking out through dark windows anymore. Not when I imagined every tiny shadow as belonging to someone with a twisted smile and a sick obsession.

My phone buzzed in my pocket, and my entire body tensed. My phone vibrating against my leg was starting to become a trigger for me. I instantly asked myself what other twisted message waited for me on the other side of my lock screen? Was he telling me that he knew we cut up the tracker? That he still had ways to find me? That I wouldn't be safe no matter how far or how fast I ran?

It was Steven texting the group chat, asking if I was doing okay after today.

I'm doing better. Thanks again for being such solid friends, you guys, I texted back and didn't have to wait long at all for a response from Steven.

Good, good. Just checking. If you need anything, I'm nearby.

How kind of him. I was going to reply, but Noah beat me to it.

Same here, Trist. We've got your back.

A flurry of yeses came in, followed by a couple of GIFs, some of them being drag queen GIFs that Noah and Colton both had a large collection of, bombarding the group with random conversations made entirely of moving images and lace-front wigs. I texted back a string of yellow hearts and hit Send, once again finding myself grateful to be surrounded by such a solid group of people. I had grown up being close to my little brother, Malik, so I understood how important family bonds were, and I could confidently say that every person in that group chat felt like family to me.

"Everything okay?" Gabriel asked, having stepped out of the bedroom and returning with the wine he had promised.

"Yeah, just texting my friends." I grabbed the glass with a thanks, clinking it with his and taking a sip. "Mmm, this is good. What is it?"

"Wine? I don't know— a pinot blanc, maybe? Is that a thing?"

"It's definitely not a thing," I said, grinning around

the glass as I took another sip.

"I'm more of a beer guy."

"So why'd you bring out the wine?"

"Because I remembered you saying red wine was your favorite. I decided to make a sacrifice tonight." He winced as he took a drink. I rolled my eyes and tried to ignore the rising hot heat inside my chest. Was he being serious? Did this man really remember my favorite drink?

It's part of his job to know things about me, I reminded myself, trying not to get carried away.

"Thanks. It's good, whatever it is."

Suddenly, I became hyperaware of the bed only a couple of feet away from me. All I had to do was set the glass down, and Gabe could push me backward, the mattress catching me as he fell on top of me.

I cleared my throat. Gabriel's eyes flicked over my shoulder before going down to the swirling red wine. "Listen, about earlier. I was serious when I said I only want to put a pause to us, not an end."

I filled my lungs with air before taking a chug. Part of me believed him, and the other part was saying, "Yeah fucking right." Once this case was over, then he'd be assigned to another one, likely somewhere other than Atlanta, and he'd jet off to his next destination where his big, muscular, Clark Kent–looking self would easily find some other boy to distract him from coming home to me.

"I'm serious," he said, likely sensing my disbelief. "Something about you has gotten under my skin, Trist. In a good way. You make me smile and laugh in ways I haven't for what feels like ages. I like being around you, not just protecting you. I don't want to ruin that, but I want to make sure I do my job right."

"I *also* want to make sure you do your job right," I teased, both of us damn well aware of the outcome of Gabe failing at his job.

His words were comforting, even though all I wanted to do was rip his clothes off and go back to exploring every single inch of him, letting him do the same with me, our bodies entwined in a dance I'd never forget the steps to.

I thought about it. Thought about tossing caution to the wind. Saying "fuck it" and going in for a kiss. After all the shit I'd been through, it felt deserved. Like blowing off a little steam with a handsome Adonis of a man was the *least* life owed me.

But life didn't owe anyone. She was the bank and the gambler. She held the cards and the chips and the entire damn casino.

Those urges, those fire-hot desires that licked at my core, were stuffed down. Snuffed out. I couldn't give in. No matter how badly I wanted Gabriel back in my mouth.

"Alright," I said, "I think I'm going to finish this and go to bed. It's been a long day."

"It has," Gabriel said. His eyes dropped to my lips. The moment froze as if encased in a sudden jet of ice, except the fire inside me kept me from freezing over. He inched closer. If he kissed me, then I'd let it go further, deeper. I'd unravel, throwing all caution out the window. We were safe here; we were together here.

We *could* be together here.

If he was thinking it, then he changed his mind. He gave a nod and a smile before saying good night. I shouldn't have felt disappointment, but the bitter pill clanged its way down my esophagus. I washed it down with a big gulp of wine.

Cabernet, I think.

Gabriel closed the bedroom door. I got my toiletries from the suitcase and went into the adjoining bathroom, finishing my wine as I got ready for bed. The entire time, I kept thinking about how Gabriel was only a room or two away from me, doing God only knew what.

At least it was better than obsessive thoughts over the serial killer trying to get me.

I finished up in the bathroom (and finished my wine), going back into the room. I glanced at the window, the blinds still drawn shut. I wasn't a fan of how close it was to the bed. It brought back childish fears of monsters breaking through and snatching me by my feet, dragging me off into the night.

Childish but not all that far from my current reality.

I swallowed down a gulp. The wine helped blunt some of the scarier thoughts. I turned on a lamp on the nightstand before turning off the overhead lights. The room was painted in a warm yellow glow. I gave a long yawn as I stretched, touching my toes and rolling my neck before climbing into bed.

Moments later was when I heard a tiny crack followed by a loud crash, and a shrill shout ripped straight out of my throat.

12

GABRIEL FERNANDEZ

I HEARD the sound and leapt out of bed, hurtling across my bedroom and ping-ponging into the hallway, going straight into the adjacent guest bedroom.

The nightstand lamp was on, but it had fallen to the floor, which made the light cast intimidating shadows on the far wall. I looked down, seeing Tristan getting up from a broken bed. The leg must have cracked and given way, nearly tossing him off the mattress.

I offered a hand and helped him up to his feet.

"I swear, Gabe, that happened just as I was laying down. It's not like I was doing jumping jacks or anything."

I laughed and felt relieved that it was just a broken bed that caused the noise. "Don't worry about it. This was one of the first pieces of furniture I ever bought. I probably should have replaced it years ago. Now I've got an excuse."

Tristan's eyes flicked downward before coming back

up to meet mine. I realized I was standing there in just my red-and-blue plaid boxers. I was in such a rush to get to Tristan's side that a shirt and sweats were the last of my worries. Tristan was also in his sleeping clothes, but that at least included a black tank top and shorts.

"I, uhm," Tristan said, clearing his throat and rubbing the back of his neck. "I'll sleep on the couch."

"No, I can take the couch. You get the bed."

"I'm not kicking you out of your own bed."

I cocked my head, amused when Tristan's eyes dropped back down for a brief moment. "We can split it, then. I've got a California king. Plenty of space."

Tristan appeared to consider the idea. For a second, I thought he was going to say no. It would likely be way too much temptation. It would go against everything we had talked about earlier.

But I really didn't want to sleep on the couch.

"Fine," he said, grabbing his pillow and phone. "Let's have a sleepover, then."

The smile grew on my face and spread to his. I tried to tamp it down, but it was useless. So instead, I turned and led Tristan over to my bedroom, turning on the light so he could get situated. I got into bed and pulled the heavy blue comforter over me, trying not to focus on Tristan's perky ass as he set up his phone and charger on the nightstand.

"Sorry about that," I said again as Tristan got into bed. The mattress dipped in his direction, as if the inanimate object was trying to push us together.

"Seriously, don't stress it. Have you seen the state of

disrepair my house is in? I wish it was just a guest bed I had to take care of."

"What's the list? Maybe we can work on it together. I'm a pretty good handyman."

Tristan chuckled at that. He got under the covers and fluffed up the pillow.

I wasn't sure what part of me was responsible for the instant boner—the primate part of my brain, the caveman part of my brain, or the highly evolved part of my brain. Likely none of them, all three parts melting away so that the lowest part of my brain could take control.

"The list is as long as a Walgreens receipt."

"You mean CVS? Walgreens aren't all that bad."

Tristan laughed again, the sound sweet enough to drink, like the most expensive bottle of wine pulled from the cellar and poured into a glass underneath a warm summer sun.

God damn, now Tristan's turning me into a writer.

"Yeah, CVS," Tristan clarified. "I don't always say the right thing on the first go—that's something you'll learn about me if you haven't already. Thank God for editors, huh?"

It was my turn to laugh. The bounce of my belly shook the head of my hard cock, pulling all my attention to the rising flames that were about to turn my bedsheets into ash. "What's at the top of the list, then?" I asked.

"Hmm, I guess my shower. I haven't had good water pressure in months. It feels like I'm showering underneath someone's piss stream."

That got a snort out of me. "I'll see if I can fix it," I

said when the laughter died down, leaving my dark bedroom back in a silky soft silence. Moonlight crept in through the drawn curtains, adding a milky white sheen to the curves of my bedposts and the dark woods of my dresser.

The silence stretched, enveloping us like the comforter that we both shared. The conversation may have died down, but the needy ache between my thighs only grew stronger, louder. I rolled over so that I was on my stomach, but that only made things worse as I stretched a leg out and pushed my hips down onto the mattress, the pressure inside me building instead of easing.

I turned back over and lay in bed, looking up at the dark ceiling, barely able to make out any of the lines in the air vent. My brain buzzed like I had drank three mugs of extra-strong coffee before getting under the covers.

And it wasn't just my brain that buzzed but my entire body. Having Tristan so close made the room feel twenty-five degrees hotter. We were separated by mere inches and a couple of flimsy articles of clothing. I could have him again, have him underneath me. I wanted to feel his cock sliding against mine. The pulsing against the comforter only proved my point. There hadn't been a man in this bed since... well, not since Christopher.

And that didn't exactly turn out well.

Christopher. My longest relationship and my most visceral fucking heartbreak. I thought he was the one. Had a ring picked out and everything. But it all came crashing down one night after a fight over some suspicious text messages.

Crashing wasn't exactly putting it lightly, either. There was a literal crash that night. One that almost ended my life, and it was because I'd been so shaken and thrown by the words Chris said to me before I got in my car.

Tristan took a heavy breath next to me. So he was still awake. Maybe we didn't have to lie here in silence, then.

"You doing alright?" I ask into the darkness.

A shuffle in the bedsheets. "Yeah, just thinking. I can't turn off."

"Same," I said.

"What are you thinking about?"

I could have lied. Said something benign. Kept things surface level between us even though all I wanted to do was dive deep into his waters.

So I didn't lie. "My last relationship, actually. I was thinking about how my ex was the last guy in here. Not that I'm comparing you two or anything. It was just one of those random thoughts that end up spiraling."

"I get it. When did you guys break up?"

Now it was my turn to take in a deep breath. I'd talked about this before with my good friends Jackson and Dean. Both of them were in the same Stonewall Elite division I was, and a couple of cases had us working together in the past. We got along extremely well, and a close friendship had formed almost instantly. They reminded me of the guys I'd fought alongside in the Marines. Hearts the size of a moon and two people I knew I could count on, no matter the time or the day.

But speaking about my ex with Tristan felt very different. We weren't in some dim bar, drinking beers and scouting the crowd for guys to help me get over Chris.

Tristan *would* be the guy to help me get over Chris. He had everything I was looking for in a perfect package —not to mention he *had* a perfect package—but with the mistakes I had already made, I needed to make sure that package remained wrapped.

At least for now.

"We broke up about two years ago," I said. "Dated for eight."

"Shit, that's a long time."

"It was. We were a great match, until things started to change. Chris was having a hard time at work, but instead of using me as a support, he used me as a punching bag. Not literally," I added as Tristan jerked up. "But we were always fighting. Shouting matches that our neighbors could definitely hear. The final straw was him telling me he had sex with one of my good friends at the time. I was livid. Stormed out of my own house, and I got in my car and drove off.

"Ten minutes later, I was upside down in a ditch, blood pouring from a cut on my forehead."

"What the fuck?" Tristan sat up this time, the bedsheets rustling. "Holy shit, I didn't know, Gabe."

"I blame myself. I should have never gotten behind the wheel that upset, but thankfully, all I got was a scar you can barely see. The scars on my heart are probably worse if I'm being honest."

"Damn, still... I'm sorry. I get what you mean about heart scars, though. I've got a few that run deep. And you can never really fix that part of you. You just have to try and find another part of your heart you can use, you can give out to people."

I looked over, seeing Tristan's shape cloaked in the shadow of midnight. The longer I looked, the more details I could make out. The rise and fall of his sexy lips, the strong bridge of his nose, the long and curving lashes that blinked open and closed. "Who broke your heart?"

He took another deep breath. I could see his chest rise and fall, his hands resting just above his heart.

"I've never had my heart broken. Not in a romantic sense. My heartbreak comes more from family... my dad. We were really close. Like really fucking close when I was growing up. He was my hero—I wanted to be a lawyer just like he was. Wanted to fix up cars and take my family on vacations and do everything that man did.

"Then I came out to him. It was my junior year of high school. He kicked me out that same day, and he hasn't spoken to me since. I went to my mom's house that night and told her everything. She gave me the longest hug and told me that she loved me no matter what, and I lived with her for the rest of my high school years."

I sat up on the bed, my eyes having adjusted, and now I was able to see Tristan clearly. There was pain reflected in those eyes, clear even in the shadows of my bedroom. "Fuck, Trist. You didn't deserve that reaction, especially not from your own father. It makes my blood fucking boil. How can you turn on your own blood like that? And a child? How in the fuckin' world—"

"It's okay, Gabe, it's okay." Tristan reached for my hand, grabbing it and squeezing it. "It made me closer with my mom. I had been so obsessed with my dad that I had missed out on a lot of time with my mom, so I felt like I got some of that back. It also made me closer with my little brother, Malik. He never got along with our dad, so when he had come out, he didn't even bother telling him."

I rubbed my thumb against Tristan's hand, the soft skin leaving sparks against mine. "Where's your mom and brother now?"

"Both in Tampa. They moved years ago, but I decided to stay here. Atlanta's always going to be my home base, no matter where life decides to take me."

"Same," I said, giving his hand a squeeze. "Tampa sounds nice, though."

"Oh, it's great. My brother works at the aquarium, and he's gotten us day passes to hang out with the dolphins. So I spend a day there and then read a book by the beach before getting some good Cuban food and having a few drinks at a nearby bar. It's really fun down there."

I nodded and settled back down into bed. Underneath the comforter, our feet briefly touched, Tristan's toes against mine. I didn't move, and neither did Tristan, not for a couple of moments, at least. And then Tristan shifted, moving his foot away from mine and snapping through the spell cast whenever our bodies connected.

He yawned and gave a stretch. I could pick up on the cue before he spoke.

"Alright, it's been a long day. I think I'm gonna try and get some sleep," he said.

"Good night, Trist."

"Night, Gabe."

The silence returned. The heat inside my core roared back to life. My cock throbbed. It pushed up at the sheets. I stretched out my legs under the comforter, feeling a tingle spread from my balls out through my body like an invisible signal.

Everything inside me shouted to roll over, to touch him, to throw the covers off the bed and watch as I made his body writhe under mine. It was a physical force, nudging me, tugging me, nearly yanking me toward him. But I resisted it.

We had decided to keep things relaxed between us, and I had to respect that. Especially since I was the one who'd suggested it in the first place.

Shit... did I fuck up?

Somehow, even with that thought clanging in my head and a constant pulse between my legs, I was still able to fall asleep.

If only I had known what was ahead. I would have done anything I possibly could to stay awake and live in that moment until the sun came up.

13

TRISTAN HALL

IT HAD TAKEN every single goddamn ounce of self-respect and self-restraint I had in me to not roll over and start humping Gabriel's leg like a horny dog. The way my body reacted when it was next to his was almost scary. Like I'd been primed to start throbbing the moment we lay down next to each other. The fact that Gabriel slept in a pair of plaid boxers and nothing else certainly didn't help my, eh, situation.

I went to sleep with an erection and woke up with one, having to take care of it in the bathroom. Before I could even start jerking off, I noticed the large bathroom window was open. It was summer, so the warm breeze was actually nice, but I didn't want any neighbors peeking over and getting a free show. Or anyone else, for that matter.

I shut the window and locked it, the frosted glass obstructing the view. I finished showering and brushing my teeth and followed the sweet scent of maple pancakes and freshly brewed coffee into Gabriel's kitchen, where he stood with his (very muscular) back toward me, his head holding his phone against his shoulder as he flipped one of the pancakes.

"Morning," I said, sitting down at the small round table next to a bright window. There was already an untouched mug of coffee at the table, still steaming, a bottle of cream and a small spoon right next to it.

"Morning, Trist. How'd you sleep?"

"Great. You've got a good mattress," I said, as if his Casper mattress was the real reason why I slept like a baby and not the fact that I had a brick wall of a man sleeping next to me.

He chuckled before going back to his phone call. "Yes, today is perfect. Thank you, Amoura. I know this is difficult, but it's important. I'll see you soon."

He hung up the call and set his phone down on the counter before turning his attention back to the grill. He scooped up the fluffy pancakes and placed them on clean white plates, adding a square of butter to each stack before drizzling them in syrup.

"That was Amoura. She's the sister to one of the Midnight Chemist's most recent victims." He set the plate down on the table, the clang of porcelain against glass sounding like a gong. I tried not to let my anxiety rise at the mention of the Midnight Chemist but couldn't help the clammy palms and tightening throat. "She's been out of the country but just got back today. Wants to talk to me."

"Does she know anything?"

"We'll find out. The cops spoke to her, but she says she's got more to share."

I arched a brow. "That she couldn't share with the police?" I cut into the pancakes, syrup and butter running down like a molten river of sweetness and calories.

"Sometimes people don't say everything to the police, even if it means saving a whole lot of people if they did. We'll see. It could be nothing." Gabriel took the seat across from me. He opted for a glass of orange juice instead of the steaming mug of coffee I clung onto like a life raft thrown into stormy waters. Every sip brought me closer and closer to shore.

Gabriel swallowed a mouthful of his breakfast before speaking again. "She has a busy day today, so she wants me there in the next hour or so. Want to go on a little field trip?"

"I actually want to stick around here if I can. I woke up feeling really inspired. I want to see if I can get some words down."

I also woke up rock hard and wishing I could kiss you, but that's for another book.

Gabriel gave me a skeptical look. He had a freshly shaven face, which made him appear equal parts younger and more intimidating. I could see the clear definition of his strong jaw, the subtle scars from a long-ago-fought battle with acne, the dark eyebrows that sat above a pair of priceless blue gems. There was nothing there to hide every tiny detail, nothing to hide the fact that I wanted to trace it all with my tongue.

"I don't think leaving you alone is a good idea," he said.

"I can't be watched twenty-four seven. And besides, I'll be here, in your home. Safe. We got rid of the tracker—he probably doesn't even know where I am now."

Gabriel took a deep breath. He set his fork down on the bright yellow place mat and drank from his Disney World cup, his Adam's apple bobbing with every gulp. "I don't know, Trist. This person's been able to surprise me, and I don't like that. I don't want you to think I'm overbearing, but I'm also worried for your safety."

"And that makes me worried for mine, *buuuut* I think I'll be okay today." I pulled out my phone from my gym shorts. "Look, why don't I text Eric and Noah. Maybe they'll swing by while you're gone? Safety in numbers, right?"

That made the tension in Gabriel's eyes ease. He went back to annihilating the pancakes. "How is it?" he asked me between bites.

"Amazing, thank you for this. For everything, really." I looked across the small table. He almost looked comically large for his small chair. He had a shirt on, but the corded muscles of his shoulders and chest appeared to be trying to remedy that. One wrong move and he'd be left wearing tattered pieces of fabric.

Well, guess that would be a right move for me.

It was weird. I could admit that. I'd never fallen so quickly for someone. And never this hard for them, either. There was an insatiable thirst that dried my mouth every time Gabriel was around me, and the only way I found I could quench it was with a kiss.

Never happened to me before. I'd dated, I had boyfriends, I had flings, I had one-night stands, and I had a fuckin' stalker.

But I'd never had this firework-in-your-chest-and-campfire-in-your-crotch kind of feeling before. Sure, some people might attribute it to a Prince Charming–type syndrome, where the armor-clad prince swoops in and saves the other dragon-cornered prince, carrying him away in his arms and having sweaty and bed-breaking sex with him in his castle. Gabriel came into my life in a similar way, fighting off the fire-breathing dragon and claiming me in every room of his modern-day castle.

But that had been a single night (and morning and part day), and now we were back to operating behind walls and boundaries. It made sense why he'd lay those down, but fuck, I hated it. All I wanted to do was explore the wild and explosive chemistry we shared together. It was the only thing that got my mind off my shitty-ass situation—and that's putting it very lightly.

We finished up eating, and I helped clean up, washing the few dishes while Gabriel put everything away. We joked as we worked, teasing each other about our wildest college stories. Gabriel had been in a frat during college and beat me with his outrageous story involving a lion statue, a purple polka-dotted thong, and a whole lot of illegally obtained alcohol.

I grabbed my laptop when our kitchen duties were up and plopped down on the couch. Gabriel came out of his bedroom wearing well-fitted light jeans and a white T-shirt, a silver chain peeking out against his tan skin. He put on a pair of sunglasses and glanced at his watch.

"How far are Eric and Noah?" he asked, standing above me. It was very difficult for me to focus on my phone when Gabe's slightly bulging crotch was at eye level with me.

"About twenty-five minutes."

It's more like an hour, but that's fine. I really didn't want Gabriel worrying about me. I understood that was part of his job, but I couldn't be babysat all day, every day.

"I'll wait, then."

"Don't," I said, setting my phone down and willing my gaze up and away from the mouthwatering package. "Don't risk losing this interview. She might know something useful."

Gabriel looked at me again, a hand in his pocket. I briefly imagined him bending down, meeting my lips with his, kissing me a quick but passionate goodbye.

He licked his lips and nodded. "Fine. Please call me for anything. Put the alarm on when I leave."

"I will."

Shit. Was he going to kiss me? Was he leaning down? Should I lean up? Should I—nope. He gave me a smile and turned to leave, closing and locking the door behind him and leaving me in complete silence. I got up from the couch and went over to the alarm system on the wall, taking off the cover and tapping in the password to set it on. It gave a reassuring beep, and a nice woman's voice alerted me that the system was armed.

There. I had nothing to worry about now. I could relax now, and I could finally get some damn words down. My deadlines were coming up, so I had to capitalize on whatever bursts of inspiration I was able to get.

Back on the couch, I put my feet up on the footstool and opened my laptop to my manuscript, imagining a bunch of virtual cobwebs being dusted away into a cloud of ones and zeroes. I read a couple of pages' worth of my previous work so I could slip back into the world. It was easy for me today, as opposed to the weeks of struggle I had previously. I played some music low in the background and got to work, letting the words flow out of me, not concerned with anything but the story and these characters.

It was cathartic. Therapeutic. I had been scared I'd lost my spark entirely, but that wasn't true, and I doubted it could ever be true. Writing was as big a part of me as my heart was. I wouldn't be here without one or the other. It was just facts—

A loud creak made my head snap up, my eyes darting to the hallway directly across from me.

What the hell was that?

I lowered the music some more. Craned my neck to the side. The sun-drenched hallway was empty, the doors to the bedrooms and bathrooms all shut.

It was probably the wind. This was an older house. It could creak at the slightest little movement. Could have been my music, too.

I replayed the song, listening for the creak.

Nothing.

Okay, so it wasn't my song. It had to be the wind. I looked over at the alarm system, the light flashing a bright ruby red. It was just me in this house, no one else. I had no reason to be scared.

Except for the fact that I was currently being targeted by a sadistic killer who had successfully murdered six gay men and women before me.

Yeah... no reason to be scared at all.

I went back to typing. The sentences formed at a slower pace now that my concentration had been broken. The words weren't flowing like they had *before* creepy thoughts of serial killers slipped into my mind.

I decided I needed a glass of water. I shut my laptop and set it down on the coffee table before I paused. The case was cracked. I never remembered dropping this laptop or even taking the case off to clean it, so how did that crack happen? It was at the corner of the smooth black plastic. I ran a thumb over it.

Another creak. I looked back to the empty hallway. Had it come from one of the bedrooms? I considered calling Gabriel but for what? A random noise in his house? Again, the alarm hadn't gone off—no one could have made their way into the house. I was alone.

Totally alone.

My attention returned to my laptop. I could have hit it against something without noticing. Unless... I pushed up at the corners of the case and popped the plastic shell off my laptop.

Something fell to the floor. It looked like a piece of paper. But it wasn't. I knew exactly what it was before I picked it up, my hand already shaking, my breakfast shooting up to get lodged in my throat.

Another tracker. He had slipped one into my laptop case, likely assuming a writer never went far without it. Fuck, shit fuck holy shit fuck. Fuuuuck!

The doorbell rang and made me jump, dropping the tracker to the floor. I hurriedly bent down and picked it up again, snapping it in half. Not like it would do me any good. The Midnight Chemist likely knew exactly where I'd been this entire time.

Shit, shit, fucking shit.

Another doorbell ring chimed through the house. It must have been Noah and Eric. I breathed a quick sigh of relief and went to the door. I glanced through the peephole just to make sure, spotting my best friends on the other side, smiling faces waiting for me.

I flipped open the alarm case and went to put in the password. But I was so shaken and scared from my discovery that I messed up the numbers. The alarm angrily beeped at me and reset itself.

"One second," I said through the door.

"No worries," Noah answered.

I tried again. It was right before I pressed the last number that a solid chunk of something connected with the back of my head and knocked me to the floor.

Lights out, curtains down. Darkness swallowed me whole.

14

GABRIEL FERNANDEZ

LEAVING Tristan alone didn't sit right with me. Instincts were shouting at me to stay, but a text from Amoura saying she was leaving town later today made me worried I'd lose whatever lead she might have provided me with. If I could unmask the Midnight Chemist, then I'd never have to worry about leaving Tristan alone again. Besides, it would only be for an hour or so until his friends arrived. It was daylight, and my alarm was set. I could open up my phone at any point and look through the exterior cameras just to put my mind at ease.

He'll be fine, I reassured myself as I pulled up to Amoura's apartment building, parking at a meter on the tree-lined street. Dusty green pollen covered some of the cars, explaining why my sniffles and sneezes were on overdrive lately. Her apartment building was an older one but well maintained, sporting a fresh paint job and a pressure-washed sidewalk. I went up to the callbox and looked for Amoura's name, tapping it and waiting for her to pick up. She buzzed me in.

The lobby wasn't as well maintained as the exterior, with a wall-to-wall mirror that had a couple of cracks in it. The beige-and-red carpet could also use some love, with a few questionable stains by the mailboxes. I walked past the elevators and went into the stairwell, going up a flight of stairs and exiting out into a dimly lit hallway.

A dog yapped from a closed door as I looked for Amoura's apartment, finding it toward the end of the hall. She didn't take long to answer. The door opened, revealing a stern-faced woman with long brown hair falling down over her tightly buttoned top. She had two colorful sleeve tattoos and an ear covered in earrings.

"Detective Fernandez?"

I put a hand out and shook hers. "Nice to meet you, Amoura. And thank you for speaking with me about Grayson."

"Yeah, of course, of course. Come in, come."

The first thing I noticed walking in was the strong scent of meat being slow-cooked somewhere nearby mixing with the smell of a little box that desperately needed cleaning. Two cats sauntered over from the couch and sat, poised like guards watching me enter.

"Sorry it's a bit of a mess in here." She picked up the gray cat and gave it a kiss on the forehead before walking us all over to the black couch. The tabby cat kept a glare on me at all times as I sat on the wooden plank cosplaying as a couch cushion.

"No need to worry about me." I pulled out my

phone and looked at her, taking in Amoura's curly dark hair and slightly frantic brown-eyed gaze. She looked like she had about a thousand things on her mind all at once, constantly worried about one thing or another. Her nails were chewed up, and her posture—perched on the edge of the couch with her hands on her knees—told me she was ready to shoot up to her feet at any moment.

"Mind if I record the conversation?" I asked.

"What for?" She bristled, her small hands collecting into fists.

"Sometimes I find things listening back to an interview that I may have missed in the moment. Nothing more than that."

She narrowed her gaze. The gray cat she had brought with us to the couch was now sitting on the armrest, looking out the window to the apartment building directly next store. "It's not a requirement," I offered her, not wanting to make her upset and cagey before this even started. That would be a quick way for me to slam directly into a dead end.

I couldn't do that. Not when the stakes were so high. Amoura could be the one lead that got us to the Midnight Chemist and ended this nightmarish saga. I had to be delicate with this. This was for Tristan, and for Amoura's brother, and for every other victim this sick fuck had taken.

Tristan...

A pang of worry entered my gut. I looked at my watch. It had been twenty minutes since I had left, so

Eric and Noah were probably getting there now. No alerts from my alarm system, either.

Still, the worry gnawed a little harder.

"That's fine, whatever." She leaned back, following her cat's gaze out the window. "It's not like I've got anything to hide."

I hit the red Record button and set it down on the scratched-up coffee table, next to a stack of magazines that looked like they'd be more at home in a dentist's office. "First, I'd like to start off with the basics: What kind of person was Grayson? What did he enjoy doing in his free time?"

Amoura kept her gaze out the window. A faint smile twitched onto her lips before disappearing. "He was amazing. The best older brother a little sister can ask for, really. He was smart—a genius, actually. And he was kind and *very* protective. He also had a big heart and a near addiction to meeting new people. It's probably what caused this all. His drive to socialize and connect."

"Did he have a big social net?"

"Huge," Amoura said, eyes turning back to me. There was a haunted look to her. A hollowness around her eyes that I hadn't noticed earlier. "He worked at a bar in a ritzy hotel in downtown. Knew all the people that would go there. Made friends with everyone, always did. Even when we were kids."

"The Mandarin, correct?"

"Yes, that's the hotel." She scratched at her neck. I noticed her eyes seemed to be darting to a semi-open drawer in the kitchen, an archway in the wall giving me a clear view. "Him and his boyfriend worked there together. That's where they met."

My head cracked to the side. "Boyfriend? Grayson was seeing someone?"

"Yes he was, but it was pretty new. I think they'd only been together for a few months before he passed."

That was news to me. Apparently, the cops didn't even dig far enough to see that Grayson was in a relationship at the time of his death. I wondered if the relationship was open or if Grayson was going behind his partner's back when he found the Midnight Chemist online.

Or maybe...

"What's his name? The boyfriend?"

She started to bite her nails, chewing pretty vigorously on her pinky. I could hear the clacking of teeth against nail. "Mason Martinez. He's probably still working there. But don't even mention my name. I don't want to get involved in this, not with whoever did it still being out there."

I wanted to point out that "getting involved" could mean the difference between saving more lives or sacrificing them like scared lambs. Instead, I nodded and decided to continue down this track. There'd be time for moral lessons later.

After I got what I needed. "Did you and Mason ever meet in person?"

"We did, a few times, yes." She spoke from behind her fingers, her words twisting as her lips tried to form shapes around the nail biting. "He seemed cool. They were happy together, which I figure is all that matters. If I'm honest, I never got the best vibe from Mason, though. It sometimes felt like his attention was elsewhere but... well, what do I know? I didn't want to get too involved."

"Now, this might seem a little intrusive, but any bit of information could help crack this open. Do you know if Grayson and Mason had an open relationship?"

Amoura let out a stiff breath. The sound of simmering meat and potatoes became fainter but still present, while the smell of dirty cat litter only seemed to intensify. *Maybe one of them took a spite shit to try and get me out of here.*

"He's had open relationships in the past," Amoura said after a short pause. Her hands were under her legs now. I didn't really clock any of her behavior as off or suspicious in any way. She was likely just an anxious person being put in the difficult situation of talking about her murdered brother. That wasn't easy for anyone to handle.

But I didn't want her getting so emotional that she shut down. I needed to shift gears.

I looked up at the clock on the wall and realized I also needed to speed things up. The longer away I was from Tristan, the worse I felt. Like an invisible tether pulled taut between the miles that separated us, getting tighter and tighter with every passing minute.

"Did your brother ever say he was meeting someone else? For coffee or drinks?"

She shook her head. Her shoulders were stiff, same as her neck. Were those tears in her eyes? Why *was* she so tense? It had been a little under a year since Grayson died. Everyone grieved on their own timelines, but she seemed to still be in the early stages of it.

"Amoura, it's okay, you can talk to me." I put on my therapist hat, sitting back and making myself as unimposing as I possibly could. I wanted to give her the space to talk because it looked like she really needed to.

She went back to chewing her nails before looking at me and letting out a heavy breath. She stood, holding her elbow tight against her body, her eyes looking everywhere but at me. For a moment, I thought that was all I would get, but she sat back down again, apologizing before explaining. "I'm just going through a hard time right now, and, well, it's my husband. Ex-husband. And you just, you look like him. That's all."

Oh. That wasn't where I thought this would go. It was never about Grayson at all.

"That's unfortunate, I'm sorry," I said, unsure of how else to handle this. It really was just an unfortunate chance that I'd walk in looking just like the man who had walked out. But I definitely wasn't going to let that be what derailed this, not when I felt like I was finally getting somewhere.

"But your brother, Amoura, did he ever mention dating someone else?"

She looked up at the ceiling, a dark yellow spot stained by an ancient leak. "He did say he was going to someone's place the day he went missing. He joked it was a little creepy over text, that the roof needed some serious work. We were supposed to go play tennis that day, but he canceled last minute."

I didn't care about how imposing or not I looked; I sat up straight and honed in on what Amoura was saying. It felt like she had been digging in the dirt and her shovel just struck gold, a loud clang sounding off to start the celebrations.

"Did he say where this house was?" I asked. It must be where the Midnight Chemist took his victims. They were never found in the same spot, but it was always in either their own homes or random Airbnb. Those places were always bare of any forensic evidence, which would be difficult to do if he were actually murdering his victims in those locations.

That led me to believe he was taking them some-where first—somewhere secluded—where he could drug and kill them once the clock struck midnight. He'd then take them to his "stage" and set them up, where he knew they'd be found days, if not hours, later.

Grayson may have gone to that house.

"I don't know," Amoura said.

"Any address, any identifier? A town, even?"

"No, I can't remember him ever mentioning exactly where. Just that the place had a busted-up red roof. He mentioned it because he said it looked like the one we used to live under as kids. I told him to get the hell out. He should have listened to me." A somber sigh left her lips.

"Those photos are of our old family house, actually.

Grayson took them. He was an amazing photographer, really."

I had to agree. I looked over to the framed black-and-white shots of their childhood home. I thought they were professional prints picked up at a museum, but hearing they were done by Grayson made me feel emotional, and I admired the way the photo was composed to show half of the home, broken but clean angles in the tilted roof and the dents in the wall, while the other half showed a large lake that glimmered and glowed even through the mono-chromatic pallet.

To die in a house that reminded him of home must have been another horrific layer to his last few hours.

That's when it hit me. Maybe he wanted to recreate that shot. "Do you still have his phone or laptop? I know it's been a little while, but—"

"I do," she said. "I have his laptop. Probably needs a charge, but I'm sure it still works. The cops looked through it already, but, yeah, maybe you might find something else. Want me to grab it for you?"

"Yes, please," I said, standing up from the couch. I didn't want to overstay my welcome. The connection between us was now established, and I felt like I got a good few pieces of information that could lead me somewhere.

Her two cats, Lacy and Macy, according to the tags hanging on their pink and black collars, both stood shoulder-to-shoulder on the windowsill, their tails flicking back and for, their bright green eyes staring daggers in my direction. They probably sensed I was a dog guy.

It didn't take long for Amoura to come back with laptop in hand. "Here you go. I couldn't find the charger, but you can probably order one online."

She was about to hand it to me when a series of vibrations yanked my attention down to my thigh. It was my phone. I wondered who was calling, asking Amoura to hold on for a second while I checked.

My heart stopped. Frozen as if dipped in liquid nitrogen. I gasped. Audibly gasped.

It wasn't a phone call or a text that took up the entire phone screen. It was an alert from my security system. There'd been a breach. The back guest bedroom window had been broken.

Someone was inside the house. Tristan, Eric, and Noah were all there, and someone had just broken in.

The ice around my heart shattered. Adrenaline flooded me as if I'd injected it directly into my veins. "I have to go. We'll be in touch." I had no time for courtesy. No time for thanks and see you laters. I took the laptop and ran out of her apartment, forgetting about the elevator and barreling into the stairwell, bouncing off the wall like a ping-pong ball as I shot down the stairs.

Two, three at a time. I flew down the stairs. This couldn't be happening. This couldn't fucking be happening. I took out my phone and dialed Tristan's number. Maybe he had gone out for drinks. Maybe his friends suggested he write somewhere else.

No answer. Just ringing. Just the pounding of blood rushing to my head. Like the roar of an all-consuming crimson tidal wave.

I burst out of the stairwell and into the dingy lobby, nearly knocking down a food delivery guy. I didn't care. Couldn't care.

All that mattered was getting to Tristan. Keeping him safe. That's all that mattered. A singular thought chasing behind me like a bloodthirsty predator:

I failed again.

15

GABRIEL FERNANDEZ

TRISTAN WAS GONE. Taken. The Midnight Chemist had him.

My heart broke. My soul sundered itself in half. I couldn't see straight past the anger and panic and fear, all boiling up inside me like the magma inside of an erupting volcano.

Eric and Noah were with me out on the front yard as my house swarmed with police. The rear window was broken, glass shards all over dirt and grass outside. Meaning the window was broken from the inside. The Midnight Chemist had already been inside my home. Stalking us like a silent predator, watching us from under the bed or through the slats of the closet door. A ghost that wanted nothing but blood.

And I gave it to him. I basically served Tristan up on a silver platter.

Noah's face was a pale white. The raw fear in his eyes was magnified tenfold by the thick glasses falling down the bridge of his nose. He stood under a tree next to me, working through his shock, watching as the police worked their way through an active crime scene.

Eric, meanwhile, spoke with one of the officers. An old friend, judging by their demeanor. I didn't have much hope for that conversation. I didn't have hope at all. This was worst-case scenario, and it was my fucking fault. I never should have left Tristan alone. Not even for a couple of minutes. I had failed, I put Tristan in danger, I...

No. I couldn't go down this road. It was self-defeating. Memories of my time in the Marines started to root themselves in the forefront of my mind. Determination and grit pushed me forward back then, when things were impossibly difficult. Even when it didn't seem like there was a way out, I kept my head up and my thoughts clear, focusing on making it out alive.

I had to do the same now. Tristan could still be saved. It had been less than an hour since the alarm went off, and it was only one o'clock in the afternoon. If the Midnight Chemist was sticking to his signature, then we had a good chunk of time before the clock struck twelve.

I still had Grayson's laptop with me. I sat down on the grass, remembering Aurora mentioning that it might need a charge. I held my breath as I opened it and pressed down on the power button. The screen remained black. I pushed the button again. Noah crouched down next to me, but his gaze was still turned toward the house, a ghastly silence hovering around him.

The screen blinked alive, made dim by the sunlight

that tried to make it past the shade of the tree towering above me.

I held my breath and waited for a password prompt. None came. The computer opened up directly into the desktop. I breathed a sigh of relief, going immediately to the photo albums.

While the colorful loading wheel spun on the screen, I decided to throw a few questions at Noah.

"So you guys were here when the alarm went off, right?"

"We were. At first, we thought Tristan had triggered it by accident. We heard him messing around with it from the other side of the door. But then it went silent for a minute or two before the alarm went off. It took us another couple of minutes to realize what was going on."

The color wheel continued to spin. The battery symbol in the top right corner was an angry red. Five percent left.

"Then what happened?"

"That's when I text the group by accident, thinking I was just texting Tristan if he was alright. When he didn't answer, Eric and I ran around the house. That's when we saw the broken window."

Still loading. Three percent. Fuck.

"Eric jumped the neighbor's fence and ran through their yard, thinking maybe they went to the street on the other side. I couldn't just stand there, so I decided to jump into the house." He looked down at his bandaged hands, some red coloring through a few spots. "I didn't even realize how badly I cut myself until the cops showed up. That was all about an hour ago, now."

Somewhere behind the tree, I heard the slam of a car door, followed by the sound of someone running through the grass. It was Yvette and Evan, both of them looking like they had changed plans from going for a jog to helping rescue their friend. Right behind them was Steven, who must have been around the neighborhood. He looked slightly disheveled, with messy hair and a slightly stained and oversized T-shirt.

"What's going on? Find anything?" Steven asked, hands stuffed in the pockets of his black sweatpants.

"Nothing," Noah answered. "Tristan's gone."

Yvette looked to the house with a hand on her heart, watching the forensics team walking in and out. FBI was here, too. Three agents that stuck to themselves and were likely just as lost as I was.

The photo albums opened to rows and rows of artsy snapshots. They appeared to have been a mix of photos taken on the phone and some with more professional cameras and more intense edits.

Maybe I won't be lost for much longer.

The number next to the battery read two percent. I didn't have all that much time left.

I scrolled through the photos, but there were tons. I had them sorted by date and looked through the most recent ones. The last photo he ever took was a stunning shot of a sunset over the Atlanta skyline, likely taken from the hotel he worked at in Downtown. It was probably this night that he'd been picked up and murdered.

But it wasn't the photo I was looking for. It felt like looking for a needle in a haystack. I scrolled: pictures of the sky, pictures of fancy drinks, pictures of cheese boards and wallpaper and antique lamps.

No pictures of a beat-up home with an old red roof.

Maybe he didn't take any photos of it. So what if it reminded him of his childhood home? That didn't make it a requirement to just take random photos and store them in the cloud—wait a second. I scrolled back down.

It was a picture of a cloudless sky, with the spindly branches of a cherry blossom tree creeping into the frame from the left, and from the right, there was the corner of a dirty and saggy roof. A red roof.

This was it. This had to be it. It was taken exactly during the time Grayson had met with the Midnight Chemist. It didn't show the entire home, but the red roof was there.

It was my only shot at finding Tristan. I clicked on the photo. The number on the corner of the screen dropped to one percent. I tapped on the "more information" button. Someone around me was talking, but I couldn't register what they were saying to me. All I cared about was the small box of metadata that appeared on the screen.

Phones didn't just capture whatever image you see on the screen. It also collected a whole shitload of other information. When the photo was taken, what settings it was taken with, how it was saved, and most importantly: where it was taken.

And there it was. An address. A street with a city and

a zip code. I immediately pulled out my phone and wrote it down.

The laptop screen blinked off, the battery sparking its last spark. It didn't matter, though. I gave the laptop to Yvette as I stood. "Hold on to that."

"What? What did you find?" Steven asked, likely sensing the sudden shift in urgency.

"You found something?" Evan echoed. This was the most expressive I'd seen him, looking worried with his big doe eyes reflecting back a heavy dose of fear.

"I've got an address."

"You do?" Noah shot to his feet. "You know where he is?"

"Possibly. I don't have time to explain right now." Every second I wasted felt like a second that took Tristan further into the grave. I had to hurry. I left to go find one of the FBI agents, the friendliest-looking one. The last thing I needed was for one of these suited-up agents to block me with their inflated egos, but I also couldn't hold this back from them. Not if it was actually the hideout of the Midnight Chemist.

"Go," Detective Arroyo said to me, turning to her partners. "I'll explain to them. Go."

She didn't need to urge me any further. I took off in a run across my front lawn, leaving behind my home to be turned over and picked through like a dead corpse, hoping to all fucking hope that I wasn't running toward another one.

16

GABRIEL FERNANDEZ

THE ADDRESS I'd gotten was about an hour away, closer to the mountains than the city, but with the speed I drove, it looked to be much less. Eric had jumped into my car at the last minute, sitting in the passenger seat under a vise of strained silence. I raced through the streets, zooming underneath yellow lights and cutting off slower drivers without remorse. There was no time to wave an apologetic hand, no time to feel bad.

All I kept seeing in my head was a tied-up Tristan, terrified and confused, wondering what the hell was going to happen to him.

I pushed down on the gas. The car's engine gave a roar as I broke the speed limit on the highway. Rush hour was only just starting, the traffic picking up.

Just ahead were two large semitrucks on either side of me. One had its blinker on to switch into my lane. They started inching in. I sped up, getting pushed back into my seat as I threaded the car through the two trucks, earning a blaring honk from the one with the blinkers.

It was dangerous, but I couldn't get stuck behind slow-driving trucks or lost tourists or frustrated commuters. I just had to get to Tristan. That was all that mattered.

Trist, fuck. I'm so sorry. I'm coming for you.

My grip tightened around the steering wheel, knuckles turned a pale white, stark against my normally tan skin. The GPS cut through my focus by announcing the exit was coming up. I jerked the wheel to the right, cutting in front of a beat-up Honda. Eric held on to the "oh-shit" handle with one hand and the center console with the other.

I may not have to apologize to the truck drivers, but I definitely had to buy Eric a beer after this.

The exit dumped us off into a run-down town on the outskirts of the Blue Ridge Mountains. An abandoned gas station seemed to serve as the spot to meet up for all the drug dealers and their customers. The street was pocked with potholes, but I didn't slow down. We were only ten minutes away, according to the GPS, and I was determined to make that in five.

The cracked road turned off into a rising hill, skinny trees encroaching on both sides, replacing the beat-up buildings and sketchy people. The houses here were tucked deep into the trees, separated by plenty of space. Mailboxes marked the dirt roads that led up to the small homes. We were almost to the destination. My heart pounded like a drum against my ribs. I was sure it couldn't be healthy, but it only got more intense as I turned down the road, a cyclone of dust kicking up behind us.

"This is it," I said, stopping the car in front of an unassuming home. It appeared normal, with white slats and a well-maintained front porch. But the red roof appeared to be needing a lot of work, and the iron bars on the windows gave an ominous hint as to what horrors went on inside those walls.

"Let's stay together," Eric said, grabbing his gun from his holster. I did the same, the heft of it in my hands acting like a comfort. If the Midnight Chemist was in there, then this nightmarish saga was about to come to an end.

We got out of the car, closing the doors as silent as possible. Gravel and rocks crunching under our feet mixed with the chorus of birds that sang all around us. I tried to pick up on any sounds of struggle or pain coming from the house but got nothing. It didn't even appear like anyone lived inside. There were no cars, no furniture on the dirty porch, no lights coming through the shut blinds.

Except that the front door was left slightly ajar. The only sign of life. Eric watched my back as I inched toward the open door. Shadows slithered through the opening. I grabbed the doorframe, slipping my fingers into the shadows, and tugged the door open slowly. The hinges gave a low creak that made me freeze. We had the element of surprise here, and I wanted to make sure we kept it.

I opened the door all the way, revealing a barren living room with a stained beige rug and a ceiling that dipped in certain places. There was enough light coming from the open door to see that there were two simple lawn chairs placed in the center of the room, facing an ancient-looking television. There was a plate with a half-eaten and extra bloody burger sitting on the floor.

Eric and I went in with our backs to each other and guns aimed outward. There was a dark hallway that curved, cutting off our line of sight. We crept toward it. My heart raced. All I wanted to do was bolt ahead, crash through every shut door until I found Tristan. I wanted to take him into my arms and tell him it would be okay, that I had him. That's all I wanted to do, but I fought that urge, my muscles straining with every small step Eric and I took, creeping deeper into the darkness.

Still no sounds. Was Tristan knocked out? Were we walking toward a trap?

No time to figure it out. Just had to act. Had to keep inching forward. It was getting harder to see the deeper we got into the hall. Eric tapped me on my shoulder and pointed in two directions. There was a closed door to my right and left. He motioned with his chin toward the one on the right. I signaled to the left.

We started to branch off. The silence only seemed to get louder, growing to a static roar inside my head. Maybe Tristan wasn't knocked out; maybe the Midnight Chemist had already pumped him with toxins.

It felt like my heart was seconds from bursting through my chest. I put a hand on the cold doorknob and used that arm to steady the one holding the gun. I looked over my shoulder, seeing Eric's outline in the darkness. He nodded.

We both threw our doors open. I aimed my gun and scanned the empty room from corner to corner. There was a slanted window that let in some light, highlighting a cloud of dust motes floating through the air. A dirty and uncovered mattress was pushed up against the wall. That's when I noticed the chain that hung down and snaked onto the mattress, heavy bolts securing it to the wall.

But no Tristan.

"Anything?" I shouted to Eric.

"There's a rug here—hold on, yeah, I found something."

I cleared my room and went to Eric, standing next to him as we looked down at a trapdoor, open to reveal a flimsy set of wooden stairs. A lightbulb hung on an exposed wire. There was a blue and purple glow that came from somewhere in the basement, past the dim yellow light of the flickering bulb.

"Tristan?" I called out, already knowing our presence would have been heard. "Tristan?"

No one responded. Only the unending silence.

"I'm going down," I said. "Stay up here and make sure no one sneaks up behind me."

"Shout if you need help."

I started down the stairs. The first one bent under my step, the next one doing the same. They protested with loud creaks. The lightbulb swung gently above my head from the cool draft.

I stepped off the last step, shocked by what I saw.

Wall to wall, sitting on plastic picnic tables, were huge tanks holding what appeared to be clown fish, swimming under the neon blue and purple tank lights. In the tanks were also anemones, which appeared to be glowing an almost nuclear green because of the lights. There was one table that looked much sturdier, set in the center of the room, sinister-looking arm and leg straps hanging off the edges. One appeared to have been torn off, sitting on the dirt-covered floor. The sound of the water filtration systems bubbled and gurgled, but no sounds of a hostage.

And no sight of Tristan, either.

Next to the table, there was a standing tray that held a variety of different syringes and surgical tools. I ran a hand over my mouth, the shock of this moment filtering in.

We'd found the Midnight Chemist's lab, but we didn't find Tristan. That meant he was still out there, at the hands of this twisted fuck, and I had no more leads. This lead should have been a case closer.

Instead, it felt like I'd run face-first into another dead end. My heart plummeted. Dropped from the height of a skyscraper, smashing onto the pavement.

"You should come down," I said to Eric as I leaned against a wooden post.

The loud creaks of the stairs sounded before Eric said, "Holy fucking shit."

He looked around, the same shock I felt flashing across his face. He let his gun drop to his side as he walked up to the tanks. There had to have been at least fifteen of them, creating a wall of bubbling blue. The sound was oddly serene compared to the morbid row of full syringes.

"This had to be where the killings took place," Eric said. "But where the hell is Tristan?"

I rubbed my forehead. Took a breath. Tried to steady my rabid heartbeat. "I don't know. He should have been here, unless the Midnight Chemist somehow figured out we were on our way and ran before we got here."

"How would they know we were on our way, though? It all happened so fast."

"Let's look around," I said, a solidifying determination taking hold. I had to keep the dark thoughts at bay. Keep my mind clear. I wasn't going to give up on Tristan. There was still a chance of saving him, and discovering the Midnight Chemist's lair could possibly push the timeline. He'd have to look for a new place to hide, and that would take time, giving us more in return.

Eric started in one corner of the room, and I went to the other.

I didn't even get started with my search before my phone started to buzz. I was close to ignoring it, but a tug in my gut told me to at least check who was calling.

It was a random number. Again, I was close to denying it, but I tapped the green button instead.

"Hello?"

"Gabriel, oh Gabe, I'm so fucking happy to hear your voice."

I nearly dropped the phone. "Tristan?"

17

TRISTAN HALL

THE TASTE of copper woke me up. What was that? Had I fallen asleep with some kind of face mask on? I couldn't remember what I was doing before I went to bed.

I tried opening my eyes, but everything was still dark. Why weren't my eyelids working? And why did that metallic taste seem to get more intense? And why did my head hurt so bad?

Realization hit me like a lightning bolt crashing down from a clear blue sky. Shock and fear flooded through me.

The Midnight Chemist had me. I'd been knocked out, and now I was blindfolded and tied down to a stiff bed, the binds around my ankles and wrists cutting into my skin. My nose must have been bleeding at some point, directing a flow of blood straight into my mouth.

No, no, no. How did this happen? It had to be a dream. A nightmare. A break in reality. It had to be—

A trailing touch against the inner part of my leg made

me jerk upward. I tried to shout, but the gag in my mouth stopped me from getting any noise out. It tasted like dirt and blood. I struggled harder against my binds, making the bed teeter back and forth.

"Shhh."

It had come from my left. I froze. Like a lamb who had stumbled into the lion's den, hearing its heavy breath inches away, hidden in darkness. Wait... Were those footsteps to my right now? He couldn't possibly have moved that quickly...

I started to plead, the words blocked by the nasty rag stuffed in my mouth. Tears wet the blindfold.

No, please. Please. I had so much more to do, so much more to see. I was just starting to get my inspiration back, doing what I loved, finding someone I could love. I didn't want to die. Please.

Please.

Please.

A series of vibrations made me freeze. Was that my phone? Maybe Gabriel was on his way. My knight in shining armor. He'd save me. He'd get me out of this.

Another touch fluttered around my neck, fingers closing around me. I stopped breathing. The fingers slowly climbed up, leaving a tingling sense of disgust against my skin as they softly brushed against my cheek, my nose. The fingers went up, over my hair, rubbing against my buzzed head. The breathing became heavier, the hand moving to cover the front of my face, as if he wanted to sculpt my face out of bloodstained clay.

I had to fight the urge to throw up. I'd drown in it, the

gag working like a dam. No. I had to stay strong. I had to stay clear-minded. I was going to get out of this.

As the hands moved down to my neck again, going under my shirt, I focused on everything but the hands. I tried to smell for anything unusual but only got the stench of body odor and dried blood. I listened for any sounds that could tell me where I was, hearing nothing but rotten breath.

But wait... no. There was something past the breathing. A bubbling. Like a filtration system in a fish tank. But it sounded like there was more than one. I heard a heavy door slide open. Like it was rubbing, brick against brick.

I filed that away, trying to ignore the hand that was now gliding over my chest. It made me want to rip off my skin. I wanted to shed it like an exoskeleton, leaving the contaminated pieces behind. Everywhere this monster touched burned. Like his fingers were iron-hot brands, leaving permanent marks wherever they touched.

More vibrations. The touch of the hand (I imagined claws at the end of those fingers) disappeared. A shuffling noise as the vibrations grew further. Footsteps that appeared to be climbing a creaky set of stairs.

A door closing. This one sounded different, further from me than the last door.

The bubbling of the water filters.

My strangled breaths.

It took me a couple of minutes until I was sure: the Midnight Chemist was gone. I was alone. Now was my chance.

I struggled against my binds, hard, using as much

force I could muster, adrenaline fueling my muscles. I grunted against the rag in my mouth, feeling the hard leather of the binds cut into my wrists. I didn't care. I pushed harder, fighting against the forces that held me down on that bed.

Something snapped on my left arm. I focused all my strength there, pulling up, fisting my hand, and tugging, grunting, crying.

Another snap, loud this time. My hand swung upward as the binds dropped off my wrists.

I immediately went for the blindfold, tearing it off before I pulled out the gag and took a deep breath of musty air before bending over the table, nearly throwing up. I held it together. I had to focus on getting out, not getting sick. I went for the other binds next, the latches easy to unclip now that I had one hand free.

I didn't even bother looking around. I wanted out. I stumbled off the table and saw a set of stairs, likely the same ones the Midnight Chemist used to leave. I ran, hurtling toward them. I didn't care that they bent under my weight; I just needed to get out. The outline of the door appeared to glow like a portal above me, light shining from the other side.

I pushed it open and climbed out before I fell to my knees.

But I still wasn't free. I couldn't slow down. I got back up and looked around, seeing I was now in an empty room, the windows boarded shut from the inside. I went for the door, not caring about all the sound I was making. The door dumped me out into a dark hallway. I went left, running, nearly tripping, gaining my footing, running faster. I saw the front door.

I flew through it, out into the sunlight. There were trees all around me. I took off into them, wanting to put that horror show of a house as far behind me as possible. I was hoping I'd find a neighbor's house, someone who could help me call for help, but I must have run in a direction that took me deeper into the surrounding woods. I started to get scared that I'd run out of one nightmare and into another—dying of exposure in some mountainous wilderness—but the tree line finally gave way and opened up onto someone's backyard.

I hurtled out of the woods like a zombie. Dirty with sticks and leaves on my clothes. I was conscious of the fact that I was likely in Northern Georgia, trespassing on someone's property, but what other choice did I have? I could keep running until I found a gas station, somewhere I could use a phone, but that meant having to potentially outrun the Midnight Chemist.

No. I had to take a risk. Had to hope whoever lived here wasn't a racist trash bag with a quick (and uneducated) trigger finger.

Instead of knocking on their kitchen window, I went around to the front door and rang the bell. The minute or so it took for them to open felt like an eternity. Like at any moment, I'd be grabbed from behind and dragged into the back of a truck.

But I wasn't. A woman in Lululemon opened the door, a water bottle in her hand, and immediately looked at me with suspicion that quickly shifted to worry, her plucked brows drawing together on her thin face.

"I'm so sorry, ma'am. I just need to use your phone. I was kidnapped."

Her eyes went wide as she pushed the door open.

"Oh Lord. Richard! This man says he needs help. Says he's been kidnapped. Bring your phone, quick!" She patted at her leggings. "Wait, I have mine here. Oh my. Here, call whoever you need."

I grabbed her fuchsia-pink phone and dialed the first number that came to mind. A number I had memorized just in case something like this ever happened.

"Hello?" His voice rang like the chorus of a dozen angels singing in my ear. It was that fucking nice.

"Gabriel, oh Gabe, I'm so fucking happy to hear your voice."

———

"JESUS FUCKING CHRIST," Noah said, a hand on the back of his neck. He leaned against the hotel dresser before Jake put an arm around his shoulder, seemingly steadying him.

I'd just finished telling the group what had happened. They were all here, gathered around me. I couldn't go home, and I definitely couldn't go back to Gabriel's house, so I got myself a room in a hotel. A room on the top floor, and not because I wanted to spend more money but because I wanted to be as far away from the ground as possible. I didn't want any chances of someone breaking in through a window while I slept.

"Here, drink some of this." Steven handed me a glass of water and sat on the edge of the bed with me, a gentle hand resting on my knee. He offered me the same kind of empathetic smile you give to someone battling terminal cancer. As if he knew this saga just wasn't going to end happily.

Or maybe that was just me projecting.

I took a sip of water before I leaned my head on Gabriel's shoulder and shut my eyes.

"Two good things came from tonight," Tia said. I looked to her, my friend still in her silk pajamas, having jumped out of bed and into the car the moment she and Jess got the call that I was okay. "One: You're here with us, safe and sound. And two: we know where the Midnight Chemist did his shit. That's got to mean it isn't much longer until they catch him. Right, Gabriel?"

All eyes in the room turned to the man sitting next to me on the bed, doubling as one of those marble coliseum columns holding me up and keeping me from collapsing. I'd never been happier to see anyone in my life than I'd been when Gabriel showed up at the door, wrapping me up tight in his big arms. I cried on his chest, his T-shirt soaked from where I had my face pressed.

And then I kissed him. It tasted like salty tears and dirt, but I didn't care. Gabe's kiss was the antidote to everything that had poisoned me. It was a spark of light in the all-consuming darkness that had been covering me like a cloak. His lips on mine pushed all that darkness back, as if he had flipped a switch and turned on all the lights.

"It definitely improves our chances," Gabriel said, looking to a stressed-out Tia, who held her can of Red Bull as if it was the only thing keeping her moored to this earth. "The FBI is clearing the scene and doing forensics tonight. I'll be getting a report this week on what they find. The agent told me I'll be allowed to go in and do my own search as well. There'll be something in there." Gabriel's hands rubbed at the center of my back.

Steven got up from the bed and went for the open bottle of vodka from the hotel tray. He poured some in his orange juice and took a chug.

"Pass that over this way," I said, holding a hand out. Steven gave me the bottle, our fingertips grazing. I held the bottle up to my lips and took a heavy swig. The taste-less vodka burned on the way down, spreading warmth through my limbs. Tonight called for drinking straight out of the bottle. "Anyone else?"

Eric reached for it. And then Colton took a shot after.

The only ones we were missing here tonight were Yvette and Eric. She had FaceTimed me to check in and apologize that she couldn't make it to the hotel. Apparently, Evan was going through something, and Yvette didn't want to leave him alone. I had told her I understood and that I'd see her tomorrow, but it did make me a little worried about this new relationship. I didn't like how Evan appeared to be separating Yvette from her friends.

"Do you have any solid leads yet?" Steven asked

Gabriel. He sat in the love seat, his back to the floor-to-ceiling window that looked out on Midtown.

"I have someone I want to talk to," Gabriel answered.

A chorus of "who?" erupted in the room.

"Mason," Gabe said. "He was one of the victims' prior boyfriends. I'm not saying he's a suspect, but he could have information. I'm hoping that after talking to him and searching the hideout, I'll have a much better idea of who's behind this."

"I just can't believe it." Jess had her arms wrapped tight around her stomach. "Trist... are you sure you're okay? After what you've been through... I just can't. My heart breaks." She sniffed back some rogue tears.

"I'm okay," I said, holding my head up and making sure there wasn't a tremble in my lip. "I really am. Shaken, yes. But *not* stirred, alright?"

That got a chuckle from the room.

"Seriously, maybe it's the shock that's still working its way through me, but I feel good. And you guys being here help with that. I'll just book an extra therapy session next month. I'll be good."

Jess shook her head but smiled. Noah clapped his hands and raised his glass. "Let's toast," he said, "to..."

"Therapy," I said, standing from the bed and getting another chuckle out of the room. "And friendship," I added with a wink. Even more laughter. We clinked our hodgepodge mix of drinks together and cheered. I looked out the window, at the twinkling lights of a sleeping city. Somewhere out there was the source of all my pain and trauma, prowling through the shadows like a wounded cat. Its claws had been dug into my chest, seconds from bearing down and ending me, but now we were the ones with the advantage. Now the hunter was the hunted, and I could smell blood in the water.

I just hoped it wasn't mine.

18

GABRIEL FERNANDEZ

THE NIGHT CREPT on as Tristan's friends slowly filtered out of the hotel room. The mood was heavy, but there was still an undercurrent of celebration to it. Tristan was safe. He got out of a situation that could have been much, *much* worse, and that was reason to pop open the champagne—which was exactly what we did. I didn't care that it was straight from the beverage display in the room and likely cost forty dollars more than it should have. Noah had brought some cups up from the lobby, and we started to unwind, the conversations shifting from serial killers to serial masterbators as Jake and Noah talked about an old coworker who got fired for being on the clock while playing with his, well, cock.

Noah's words, not mine.

I sat on the edge of the bed, not leaving Tristan's side. His leg against mine was a comfort I didn't realize I needed.

Tia and Jess were the first to say their goodbyes.

Noah and Jake left shortly after, Eric, Colton, and Steven being the last three standing. Eric sat at the small round table in the corner of the room, the nearly empty bottle of champagne next to his cup, Colton at his side. Steven sat across from them, mindlessly shuffling a deck of cards as he looked out the window and down to the street. There was a bright floor lamp that appeared to be shining a spotlight onto Steven, highlighting a face that appeared to be smoothed over by a filter. Whatever makeup techniques Steven used deserved to be studied.

Eric stretched out his legs and reached an arm over Colton's shoulders.

"Thank you, guys, for keeping me company tonight," Tristan said, gaze trailing down to his feet, bare against the dark blue hotel carpet. "I don't know how I would have gotten through it. I know I still have a lot of processing to do, but I'm just glad to be here with you guys." He looked up at me, his golden-brown eyes appearing even lighter to me. He had eyes I could stare into for hours. Like gems locked up behind protective glass, a thousand different glittering facets drawing me in.

How had I ever been able to resist him? From the moment I laid eyes on Tristan, I knew it had been game over. He checked off every box underneath "the perfect man."

And I almost lost him. I would have never had the chance to tell him how perfect he really was.

That changed tonight. I wanted Tristan to know that I was done playing games. Life could be cut short in the blink of an eye. Holding back my true feelings for him didn't keep him safe, so I was done holding anything back. Tristan would know exactly how I felt about him before the sun came up.

Eric sat up, an easy smile on his face. He wore a *Black Panther* T-shirt, his beard coming in thick on his face, a silver necklace glittering on his neck. "We're glad to be here."

"Yeah, honestly, I needed a distraction. Not that I wouldn't have taken literally any other distraction in the world, for the record." Colton swirled his cup and took a sip before speaking.

"What happened to you?" Steven asked.

"My dad came out to me today."

All of our attention whipped to Colton.

"Oh shit. Really?" Tristan asked. Steven leaned forward, holding his cup with both hands, eyes wide, stare intense. "How was that?"

"It was fine. The only big issue was that he told me he realized when he hooked up with my mom's lawyer, who also happens to be my sister's now husband. And she doesn't know."

My face wasn't normally very expressive, but I felt it crack, my jaw dropping open and my eyebrows jerking toward the ceiling.

"That's... shit. That's messy," Tristan said.

"Yup. He was going to tell me while we were at our family retreat, but considering everything else going on, he figured he would wait for a better time. Family, huh?"

I thought about my relatively uncomplicated family. Mom worked at an airport, and my stepdad worked as a truck driver, neither of their sides of the family causing any issues. No one was in jail or begging for money or stealing from someone else. Everyone got along at Thanksgiving and Christmas. It made me grateful, but it also made me miss them. I made it a point to visit them in North Carolina at least once a year, but it had been two since I'd last seen my parents.

"I told him that it was all going to be fine," Colton continued. "Told him that I loved him and that if he needed any random tips about being gay, then to ask me."

Eric smiled and put his hand on his husband's leg. "You're a good son."

"He's been a good dad."

"What kind of tips do you think he'll need?" Tristan asked, leaning back on the bed. He seemed to be getting more and more relaxed as the night wore on. I knew he'd need a lot more time to fully process what had happened to him, but the return of his easygoing smile so soon after he'd been abducted felt like a good sign.

"Well, for starters, my dad has terrible taste in men if he was going after that douchebag lawyer, so I'll have to make sure he finds a good guy to settle down with. Plus, he'll probably need help figuring out which *Housewives* franchise to watch. It's a whole new world."

Eric laughed and arched a brow. "Do you even watch any of the *Housewives*?"

"No, never have and probably never will. But that's why I'd ask Noah. I think he has some of those episodes memorized." He gave a stretch and a yawn.

"My family life would put an entire season of that

show to shame." Steven looked down at his chewed-up fingernails. A shadow of some heavy memories appeared on his expression, his eyes hooded by heavy lids. As if he were feeling a physical pain.

"What happened?" Tristan asked, head cocked.

Steven shook his head, looked out the window. "What didn't happen?" He took a rattling breath before releasing it in a cough, covering it with his elbow. "My father was... he was a monster. And I don't say that as an expression. He was a literal monster. He abused my mom and my sister until she woke up in the middle of the night and ran off. She took Hazel with her, but she left me."

My jaw dropped open. Tristan put a hand over his mouth.

"I haven't talked to her since. I know she did it because she felt like she couldn't raise two kids on her own. I was older by seven years. But... well, she left me with him. He would treat me like an animal, but it got even worse when he found out I was gay. That's when he'd lock me in a closet for days at a time. When I outgrew the closet, he would lock me up in the spare room. All I'd have was a fish tank to keep me company. I got so thirsty once I had to drink out of it." Steven had soundless tears sliding down his face. My heart broke for him. How could anyone treat their own flesh and blood like that?

Steven was right. His father was a literal monster.

"Jesus... fuck." Colton reached over and grabbed Steven's wrist. "I'm so sorry."

Steven tried to muster a smile, but it was a shaky one.

"Do you know where your sister and mom are now?" Colton asked.

"Nope. No idea. I tried finding them. Even hired a PI to do some digging, but they couldn't find anything. And that's okay. I made it through without them. I can keep on making it through."

"Damn right," I said. "No one should go through what you've been through, Steven, but just from knowing you these past few weeks, I can see that you fought your way out of that situation and kept your sanity. That's extremely difficult to do."

He nodded, and the ghost of a smile flickered onto his face. "I have my moments."

"We all do," Tristan said.

The conversation slowed down as we all digested the bomb that Steven had dropped. Exhaustion hung heavy in the air as the day started catching up to us. A lot had happened, and it would all need unpacking, but not tonight. Things were still too fresh. Too raw.

Tristan gave a stretch and a yawn, which seemed to jump around the rest of the group in rapid succession. Eric pushed his chair back when he finished with his stretch.

"Alright, you guys, I think it's time for us to head home."

Eric jingled the keys in his pocket and stood up. Tristan and I stood to meet them at eye level. Eric wrapped his best friend into a tight hug, joined by Colton. When they separated, I could see that both Eric's and Tristan's eyes were glistening.

"I love you, Trist. If you need anything, give us a call."

"Thanks, Eric. I'll send up the bear signal if we need anything."

Eric winked and reached for Colton's hand. They were gone moments later, leaving just me, Tristan, and Steven as the last men standing.

Tristan sat on the bed, his back against the head-board, his legs crossed underneath him. I didn't want to be rude, but it was getting late, and I was ready for it to just be Tristan and me, but instead of getting up to leave, Steven moved over to the love seat and appeared to make himself more comfortable. He threw a blanket over himself and smiled at us, his gaze lingering on me before jumping to Tristan.

"Do you guys want to play a game?" He looked over at the deck of cards on the table. "I'm still buzzing. All this adrenaline tonight has me thinking I won't be sleeping."

Tristan shot me a subtle glance before offering a strained smile. "I don't think I'm up for another round."

Please get the hint. Please get the hint.

"That's fine," he said, moving the blanket off himself and going to stand.

Oh, thank God.

He got up, but instead of going for his shoes by the door, he went to the bathroom. Tristan mouthed the words "I'm sorry" to me, likely sensing the growing exhaustion.

"It's fine," I mouthed back. I really didn't mind. After

how he'd opened up to us earlier, I was fine with him staying a little longer to decompress. Steven was in the bathroom for less than a minute before he came back out, scratching his nose on the way to the love seat, passing his dirty sneakers without a second glance.

"What time is it?" I asked, as if I didn't already know it was eleven forty-five at night.

"Eleven forty-five," Steven cheerily answered after checking his watch.

"Are you normally a night owl?" Tristan asked.

"Not normally, no." His smile curved at the corners, almost like that of the Cheshire cat. "I'm just not tired. Guess it's all this excitement."

"Guess so," Tristan said. He sucked in a breath before blurting out, "I'm exhausted as fuck, though." His eyes opened wide before he amended with "Sorry, that was blunt. I'm just feeling it now, Steven. I'm like five seconds away from passing out."

Steven's smile curled downward. "No, I get it." Those dark brown eyes flitted in my direction. "You sure you guys don't want to play another round? I can get us more drinks. Pizza?"

Tristan pursed his lips. I jumped in, realizing he might need an assist. "I'm pretty tired, too. It's been a long day."

"It has," Steven said, starting to stand. "It really has."

"Thanks for coming by." Tristan stood and opened his arms for a hug, which Steven quickly fell into. He shut his eyes and rested his head on Tristan's shoulder. It looked like a hug from a childhood friend who hadn't seen you in years.

"I'm glad you're okay," Steven said when they separated.

"Me too," Tristan deadpanned, pulling a laugh from both of us. I stood and shook Steven's hand, my fingers dwarfing his.

"Have a great night, boys."

"You too," I said, walking him toward the door. He gave one last lingering look over his shoulder before leaving. I had the impression that he wanted to stay much longer, but I had to admit that closing the door and being left with just Tristan and me was exactly what I wanted.

Tristan offered me a growing smile as I went over to his side, sitting down on the edge of the bed next to him. I planted my feet firmly on the carpet and looked out the floor-to-ceiling window. "How are you feeling?" I asked, watching as the multicolored lights of the city twinkled underneath us, dancing with the few stars that were strong enough to make it through the light pollution.

"Like I was kidnapped and nearly killed by a sadistic monster but somehow managed to survive and escape. So... alright, I guess?"

I chuckled at Tristan's dark joke, turning my gaze to him and placing a hand on his foot. He smiled at me. "In all seriousness, I'm not sure how I'm feeling. Relieved. Scared. Happy. Nervous about the future. Glad that you're here. Worried. Basically, I'm feeling everything, everywhere, all at once."

I squeezed Tristan's foot, offering him a smile that matched his.

"Also, kind of horny. But that's weird. Right?"

Another laugh escaped me. I rubbed my thumb along the tops of his toes. "You're allowed to feel however you feel without it being weird. I think an increase in sex drive is linked to adrenaline, anyway. In case you wanted a scientific explanation for why you wanted to jump my bones right now."

"Gotcha. Yeah, that does make sense." Tristan leaned in and gave me a kiss. "I feel like I need to shower. Wash all of today's shit off me."

"Go," I said. The fluttering sensation of his lips against mine didn't disappear just because the kiss broke. "I'll be right here."

"Promise?"

"I'm not going anywhere. Promise."

He kissed me again, the flutters cascading down my spine, spreading through me like a flowing river, filling my crevices and parching my drought. Something about that kiss solidified what I felt for Tristan, and I was determined to put that feeling to words tonight.

19

TRISTAN HALL

THE WARM WATER hit my back with a pleasant force. I rolled my neck, letting the water fall over my face, my neck, my chest. I tried to picture myself on a deserted island, inside of a beautiful villa with a naked Gabriel, both of us hundreds and hundreds of miles away from all our problems, all our trauma, all our demons. Just the two of us, getting lost with each other. God damn. That's all I wanted. I'd give it all up if it meant that's what I'd get.

I'd give up my books, my career, my entire fucking life.

At some point, not sure when, tears started to mix with the water from the shower. I looked down at my wrists, seeing the faint marks from where the ropes had been tied, and I cried even harder. Realization hit me like a hurricane, nearly barreling me over.

I was so close to death. The Grim Reaper had their scythe held up right against my neck. And it still wasn't over. Whoever took me was still out there, and I wouldn't be able to stop looking over my shoulder until they were caught.

More tears. I crouched down, letting the water pound into my back and my neck. I let it all out. A mixture of fear and panic and dread, but also relief and hope and determination. I'd never felt this wide range of emotions all at once before. It would probably come in handy for my writing later, but right now, I was shocked my body could even process all of this.

Shock. There's another emotion to add to the list.

After about thirty minutes of just letting the water fall on me, I figured it was time for me to get out before Gabe started to worry. I turned off the shower and grabbed one of the hotel's plush white towels. Maybe it was the fact that I'd been kidnapped hours before, but something about today made me appreciate just how goddamned soft the towel was. I held it against my face and nearly started to cry again.

I wasn't always so emotional, but I figured this was probably expected after everything I'd been through.

Gabriel was lying on the bed when I walked out, the towel wrapped around my waist. I went for my suitcase and grabbed a pair of black boxers, changing in the bathroom before walking out again. Gabriel had changed, too, wearing a white tank top and gray shorts that looked like they were fighting against his big thighs for their dear life.

"How was the shower?" Gabe asked.

"It was everything I needed." I walked over to the

window, wondering if my eyes were still puffy from all the crying. The city underneath us seemed so inviting. It was the weekend, so Atlanta was alive with people going out to dance and drink at the clubs and bars. I wondered how many of them were concerned about the rabid serial killer still on the loose out there.

I pulled myself away from the window before my thoughts could spiral. Gabe patted the side of the bed. I padded my way over, lying down with plenty of space between us.

Space I found that I instantly hated.

"What a fucking day," I said, looking up at the ceiling. "I'm just... I'm fucking tired."

"You've been through hell and back today."

"Fuckin' literally." A familiar and unwelcome pressure built up in my throat. I took a deep breath and tried to swallow it down, but that only made it worse. The cry came out strangled. "Sorry."

"Trist, you don't have to apologize. At all. Let it all out. That's the best way to deal with this."

"I already let most of it out in the shower," I said, rubbing away the streak of moisture that appeared on my cheek.

"You'd be surprised how much more is left." Gabe offered me a warm smile. His blue eyes were bright with something I couldn't quite pinpoint. Hope? Happiness? He was close enough that I could smell the faint touch of the leathery cologne he liked to wear. Manly and strong and inviting. I crossed my legs at the ankle and looked back out the window, trying to ignore the warm spark that planted itself somewhere between my ribs.

I didn't want to talk about me anymore. There would be time to deal with my shit. "Steven's story was pretty wild, huh?" I asked, steering the topic away from me.

"It was. You never know what someone's going through, huh? He's always smiling and joking around. Never giving any sign he's carrying all that trauma around with him." Gabe stretched his arms over his head and let out a low yawn. I couldn't help but glance sideways at Gabriel's pits.

How was every single part of him so fuckin' perfect? And why did I have the urge to lean over and stick my face directly into his underarm?

Maybe it's still all the adrenaline inside me.

Yeah, that had to be it.

Gabe shook his head and looked to me. "I just can't believe there's a person out there who would hurt their own child like that. It doesn't compute for me. I've seen a lot of shit, being a Marine and working in the field I do, and I've got to say that evil parents are some of the worst monsters out there. A kid should be able to trust their parent before anyone else."

"That's so true," I said. "But then look at my dad. He tossed me and my brother to the side because we were gay... What about your parents? I don't think we've ever talked about them."

"They're good parents, just not a good match." I sensed a shift in Gabe's tone. His words got lower, his voice carrying something with it. Like a bag of pebbles being dragged over the sidewalk. "Opposites on every level. They'd fight constantly. I'd hear them through the walls, talking about how I was the only thing keeping them together. It was a lot to hear as an eight-year-old. A lot of pressure, a lot of sadness and worry. It lasted until they finally split up when I was twelve."

I leaned a little closer to him. "Damn, that is hard. I'm sorry."

"You and your apologies." He shot me a wink. "Thanks. I made it through, though. So did my parents. It got rocky, definitely. Toxic and dark. Lots of shouting and broken dishes, but they never hurt each other. Not physically, at least."

"Sometimes the mental scars could be just as bad as the physical."

"Ain't that the truth."

Gabriel smiled, the darkening beard hiding that one dimple on his face that usually made an appearance when he was clean-shaven. It was wild to me how I already knew the geography of his face—and not just his face. Memories rushed back to me, of having him underneath me, his tongue against my hole and his cock throbbing for my touch. If I had a piece of paper, I might be able to draw out the exact shape of him.

Well... maybe not draw. I was always a terrible artist. But I could write the shit out of that scene.

And now I knew a little more about him. Not just about his body but about his soul. He didn't have to share himself like that with me. We were nothing but bodyguard and client. *Maybe* friend and friend. But nothing more than that, and that's how we decided it should be. It was a mutual choice, and I had to respect it.

But *fuck* did I want to be between his legs right now.

Is that normal? Shouldn't I just want to be going to sleep right now?

No. I didn't want to sleep tonight. I wanted to live tonight. Wanted to feel what it meant to be alive. To celebrate the fact that my heart still beat and to make that heart pound a little faster.

"Tired?" Gabriel asked as if reading my mind.

"Actually the opposite." I sat up, leaning back on the headboard. A heavy door slammed somewhere in the hallway. "I'm still buzzing. I don't know. I feel like I can run a marathon. That's weird, right?"

"No, it's not weird at all." His voice was low again. This time, I picked up on a subtle growl. Like there was a caged tiger waiting inside of him, wanting to come out.

"Alright, good. Because I'm fuckin' spinning right now. I don't know which way is up or down. All I know is that I'm glad you're here with me right now."

"I wouldn't want to be anywhere else," he said, which wasn't exactly something a bodyguard was expected to say. My heart rate sped up, and I became very aware of just how close our feet were to each other. I decided to say, "Fuck it," and I shifted so that my foot was directly against the top of Gabe's.

Skin to skin, heat to heat. The contact made my entire body flush with warmth. For a second, I worried he would move away, but he stayed with his foot under mine, our legs close together, my boxers beginning to feel more and more restrictive.

"I, uh…" My words trailed off as my gaze dropped to Gabe's big lips, pink and slightly pouty and so fucking perfect.

He licked them, a smirk lifting the corners. His eyes fell to my mouth, and his smirk turned into a smolder. The room felt about five hundred degrees hotter.

"Gabe, I know we've talked about us keeping things professionally, but, I dunno, it's getting harder and harder."

"Oh, it is?" he asked suggestively.

I smiled, grabbing my bulge and giving myself a stroke. "It is."

That was all he needed. The green light. Gabriel pushed in, those plush lips of his finding a home against mine, the kiss crashing over me like a warm wave from a crystal-blue Caribbean beach. Refreshing and revitalizing.

Gabriel's kiss was an antidote, his touch the cure. My life had felt like it had come undone hours earlier, but Gabriel's hand on my neck and his tongue in my mouth knit it all back together again. I sunk into the feeling, letting my body go, releasing the insane amount of tension that had built up around my shoulders and back, melting into this moment. No worries, no stress, no fear.

Just us.

I breathed him in, trying to memorize his taste, the way his tongue danced against mine. The ghost of the champagne we drank warmed my muscles and helped me relax even more, letting Gabriel guide me so that I was lying down, lips still locked, Gabriel's heavy body weight coming down onto me. His legs went between mine and opened them, his hand still cupping the back of my neck as our kiss grew, the flame fed by the mutual throbs between our legs.

I was already rock hard, and Gabriel wasn't shy about letting me know he was too. But there was a pause in our dance, a brief intermission as Gabriel broke the kiss and looked down into my eyes, searching for something.

"You're okay with this, right?" he asked.

I licked my lips and rolled my hips, rubbing myself against him. "I'm very okay with this. It's exactly what I need."

You're exactly what I need. The thought rooted itself inside me, right next to the burning desire that made its home inside my core. I'd figure it out later. There were other things I wanted to focus on for the moment.

"Are you?" I asked, my hands rubbing underneath Gabe's tank top, feeling the strong muscles that twitched with every movement.

"I am, yes." He came down again, crashing his lips with mine. The swell of passion swept me up and pulled me offshore. My hands gripped Gabriel's strong shoulders, his weight feeling like the most comforting thing in the world. I felt safe with his arms encasing me, his heart beating only inches from mine.

I rutted against him, the pressure inside my balls building. "These clothes need to come off," I said through a breathy moan. "I need to feel your big cock against mine. Fuck, Gabe. I need to feel it inside me."

Gabriel's blue eyes swirled with a solar kind of heat, warming those waters and inviting me to dive in headfirst.

And that's exactly what I intended to do.

20

GABRIEL FERNANDEZ

TRISTAN'S WORDS hung in the air, heavy with anticipation. I gazed into his eyes, searching for any sign of doubt or hesitation. He'd been through so much today. I would have been completely fine calling it a night and cuddling with him, but I certainly wasn't complaining about this, either. His sultry and smoldering gaze met mine, unwavering and filled with an intensity that made my breath hitch for a moment. "Are you sure, Trist?" I asked softly, my voice barely a whisper.

Tristan's lips curved into a gentle smile. "Yes, Gabe. I'm sure. I want this... I want you."

With a nod of agreement, I pulled away just enough to remove my tank top, revealing my chiseled chest and abs. I watched as Tristan's eyes widened, taking in every detail of my body. His reaction to me made my pulse quicken, and I could feel my own arousal pressing against the fabric of my shorts, leaking enough to create a dark spot.

"You're... incredible," Tristan whispered, his voice filled with awe.

My body warmed at his words, but I didn't want to be the only one exposed. "Your turn," I encouraged him, my voice soft but insistent, my gaze dropping down to the boxers that could barely contain his erection.

Raising his hips, Tristan slid his boxers off, revealing his own lithe and toned body. Our eyes locked, and I could see the desire and vulnerability in his gaze. I knew I needed to be careful, but I also knew that we both craved the intimacy and connection that came with being so close to one another. We had set up boundaries before, but they were all meaningless now. I wanted to barrel through any kind of wall or defense we had in place, reaching the center of Tristan and making him mine.

Only mine.

I pressed my needy body against his, making our cocks brush against each other. Tristan's breath hitched, and I could see a flash of fear in his eyes. I paused, cupping his face gently in my hands. "We don't have to do anything you're not comfortable with," I reassured him. "Just say the word, and we'll stop. We can keep things chill tonight."

Tristan closed his eyes and took a deep breath, steadying himself. When he opened them again, the fear had been replaced with a fiery heat. Or maybe there was never fear there in the first place. "I trust you, Gabe," he murmured. "I want this. With you. Fuck being chill. I want you to wreck me. Make me shout your name while you fuck my brains out."

His words were the equivalent of dumping a bucket of pure gasoline onto an already roaring bonfire.

Our mouths met in a passionate kiss, and any lingering doubts were swept away in the heat of the moment. The sensation of skin on skin was electrifying, and I could feel every inch of him reacting to my touch. Our hands explored each other's bodies, tracing every curve and muscle, as if we were trying to memorize every detail.

Tristan's breath hitched in his throat, his hands moving to cup my ass, pulling me down onto him so that our stiff cocks rubbed together. He whispered into my ear, "Gabe, please, I need you inside me."

Hearing him say that sent a thunderous shiver down my spine, and I knew I couldn't deny him what he needed. I went and grabbed the lube, squirting some in my palm and stroking it over my throbbing cock. Tristan watched me, a lazy hand jerking himself off, his eyes filled with anticipation and need.

"Are you sure you're ready?" I asked him one more time, wanting to be absolutely positive he was comfortable with what was about to happen.

Tristan nodded, his eyes never leaving mine. "I'm ready, Gabe."

I positioned myself between his legs, spreading the lube around his tight hole. His breath quickened as I slowly pushed my fingers inside him, making sure he was ready for me. I met some resistance, his hole clenching around me.

"Breathe, that's it. Relax."

As I felt him let go and open up for me, I pushed my finger in deeper, watching it disappear inside of him. He gasped as I curled it upward, rubbing against his swollen prostate. His thick cock leaked a string of precome out from the tip. I used my free hand to rub my thumb over his wet dick, bringing that precome up to my lips and sucking my thumb clean. It tasted sweet and salty and just like Tristan.

All it took was one hit and I was hooked to his taste.

"*Fuuuuuuck*," Tristan exclaimed as I pushed in another finger. His eyes locked with mine as I worked him open, probing him, his velvet hot heat encasing my fingers and making me wish it was my cock instead.

When he started to grind down on my hand, begging for more, I knew it was time.

"I'm on PrEP," I said as I pulled out my fingers and replaced them with the head of my swollen cock. "Tested last week, and everything was negative."

"Same here," Tristan said, rocking his hips so that the tip of my dick slipped inside of him, pulling chesty moans from the both of us.

Our eyes met, and with a nod of affirmation from Tristan, I pushed forward, slowly entering him. I watched as his eyes fluttered shut, his lips parting in a moan of pleasure and relief.

"Are you okay?" I asked, concern lacing my voice.

Tristan nodded, his breath coming in shallow gasps. "Yes... fuck, it feels amazing."

With that encouragement, I began to move, slowly at first, giving Tristan time to adjust to the sensation of being filled by me. His breaths grew deeper, his moans more insistent, and I could feel the heat of his body meeting mine. His legs wrapped around my waist, pulling me closer, urging me on. His balls were so fucking tight they looked ready to bust with only a couple more thrusts.

"Fuck, Trist, your hole feels so fucking good. I'm in heaven. Fuck."

As our rhythm increased, Tristan's hands clutched at my back, his nails leaving trails of scarlet-red desire across my skin. I bent down to capture his lips in another searing kiss, our tongues tangling together as our bodies moved in unison, finding the beat to a song only our hearts could hear.

The room filled with the sounds of our passion, our moans and gasps echoing off the walls as we moved faster, more urgently. Our eyes remained locked, the connection between us as strong and intense as the physical sensations we shared.

I could feel the pressure building within me, and I knew I couldn't hold back much longer. "Tristan," I gasped, my voice breaking as I tried to maintain control. "I'm close."

Tristan's eyes fluttered open, and his gaze met mine. "Me too, Gabe," he whispered breathlessly. "Please, do it. Fill me, Gabe."

The permission I needed, the encouragement I craved, was enough to push me over the edge. With a final, powerful thrust, I felt myself reach the point of no return. My vision blurred as pleasure ripped through me, my body shaking with the intensity of my orgasm. Tristan's own climax followed, his cries of ecstasy mingling with mine as we rode out the waves of pleasure together, riding up into the clouds that drifted over the quiet city. Ropes of come shot from his dick, landing on his chest and belly, covering his dark skin in dripping white.

"Holy... fuck," I said, trying to catch my breath as my vision returned.

"Wow" was all Tristan could muster, sweat beading across his forehead.

Once the aftershocks subsided, I gently pulled out and collapsed next to Tristan, both of us gasping for air. I somehow managed to muster the strength to get up and grab a moist towel and went back to clean off Tristan, gently rubbing away the come. He watched with a smile on his face, his body completely relaxed.

"You're so fucking beautiful," I said, bending down to kiss his chest, his salty release still lingering on his skin.

"Says the Adonis," Tristan replied, his hands tracing soft circles across my shoulders.

"Seriously," I said, kissing up toward his neck. Salt and come mixed on my tongue. I ran my tongue across Tristan's jaw, his stubble scratching me as he shivered underneath me.

That was all my spent body could muster before I collapsed next to him. He nestled into me like it was the most natural thing in the world. Just two men, floating together across space and time, creating their own little bubble of paradise, even if the sun was guaranteed to pop it when it rose in the morning.

As we lay there, wrapped up in each other, I knew that we had crossed a threshold, moving from friends to something deeper, something more profound. Our connection had only grown stronger, and it was time I stopped denying it.

Time to make it real. "Let's be boyfriends," I said, the words solidifying in the air before they had a chance to solidify in my brain.

A moment of dragged-out silence before Tristan spoke. "I was hoping that's where this was leading."

"You were?"

"Of course. I've told you before I never really had an actual relationship. I don't think I ever found someone that really lit up that spark. But fucking hell, you lit that spark the second we met. I swear. It's been so hard trying to fight it."

I reached down and palmed him in my hand, grinning. "I can tell how hard it's been."

"Fucker," Tristan said, leaning in and nipping on my bottom lip. My palm came back wet from his still-leaking cock. "What about the rules?"

"Screw the rules," I answered. "They were all made up anyway. But I know you're real. This is real. What I feel for you is real, Trist. And I'm ready to sink into it."

He looked at me with those soft brown eyes that could melt an iceberg. "Me too," he said, kissing me, climbing back on top of me, both of us getting hard again.

We went for another round, this one infinitely better

than the last, if only because when I looked down, I wasn't just looking into Tristan's eyes; I was rocking my hips into my boyfriend, watching him writhe in pleasure as he begged for more.

And that's exactly what I gave him.

21

TRISTAN HALL

THE HOTEL ROOM looked like a cyclone had escaped out of my luggage. Clothes hung half off the lip of the suitcase, as if it was regurgitating a pair of boxers and a couple of T-shirts. Jeans hung off the back of a chair, and a dirty pile of clothes was beginning to form on the desk. I stretched out on top of the bed, curling into a still-napping Gabriel, the afternoon sun sending a warm golden ray across my bare legs. Gabriel's phone buzzed across the nightstand.

Life felt different in the days after the kidnapping.

Bottled water tasted like it came from a fresh Fiji spring (and I hated water). Television and social media took a very low spot on my list of priorities (and they used to be high as fuck). I was equal parts hungry enough to eat an entire buffet and also full enough to munch on popcorn for the rest of my life.

And the sex. The sex was out-of-this-fucking-world. The kind of sex that made your toes curl, eyes roll, and brain melt all before you even come. Maybe some of that had to do with the fact that it was Gabriel who was tossing and flipping me around on the bed like I was some kind of toy, but I think a lot of it came from being at one of my most extreme and frightening lows only to be thrown as close to the sun as possible, the heat working to burn away any fear and anxieties that were nipping at my heels.

And, oddly enough, the words were flowing better than ever. I had woken up early these last few days and gone down to the hotel cafe, which had a really nice view of the flower-filled courtyard. I sat at a table and started typing away. Plot holes that had been fighting me for months now seemed to sort themselves out. Character arcs were completed, and tensions were heightened.

At one point, I was chuckling to myself, thinking that maybe I needed to get kidnapped more often.

That thought quickly sent me on a small spiral and had me coming back up to the room, where I found Gabriel in bed, one leg out of the covers, his mouth slightly open, his chest slowly rising and falling. I didn't care that I'd already had two cups of coffee. I stripped down to my boxers and climbed back into bed, curling into Gabriel's solid form as we both drifted back off to sleep.

Gabe's phone continued to vibrate. He yawned and grabbed it, sitting up when he realized it was a FaceTime call.

"Shit, it's Zane. Probably about the case." He looked over at me. "You're decent?"

"Just don't tilt the camera down and we should be good," I answered with a grin. The sheets tented with my erection. I couldn't help it. Cuddling with Gabe was an extremely potent aphrodisiac.

And judging by the neighboring tent next to me, cuddling with me was just as potent.

"Hey, Zane, what's up?"

A handsome man's face filled the screen. He looked like he had just gotten out of a New York City subway. A flow of people surrounded him as gigantic pillars of glass and metal stretched up toward the sky behind him. Gabriel held the phone at an angle so that it was just his face in frame.

"This a good time?" Zane asked.

"Yeah, just waking up from a nap."

I smirked as I reached over and stroked Gabriel's hard dick through the sheets. His face didn't give anything away. I started to shift in the bed, my mouth starting to water.

"It'll be quick, but I don't think you're going back to sleep anytime soon. I got you access to the Midnight Chemist's hideout."

All thoughts of sucking dick dissolved, my mouth drying up quicker than a puddle sitting directly underneath the hot sun.

Gabriel sat up, his focus pinned onto the phone screen. "When?"

"Now. You've got two hours. Go and look for anything that can help crack this."

Gabriel threw off the bedsheets and was already

getting out of bed. "Thanks, Zane. These cops were stonewalling the shit out of me."

"We're not called Stonewall Investigations for nothing," Zane replied with a chuckle. A series of loud honks from somewhere off-screen sounded throughout the hotel room. I half expected to hear someone shout, "Ey, I'm walkin' here!"

"Call me with anything you find," Zane said. "And you're sure you don't need any backup, right?"

Gabriel paused. Chewed on his lower lip before shaking his head. "Yeah, I've got this. I'll let you know how the search goes."

Gabriel hung up the call and went back to pulling on his shorts, zipping them up, and turning to me. "This could be big."

I bit back a joke about how it was already big. Gabe was right. The Midnight Chemist didn't have a chance to go and clean out his hideout before it was discovered, which meant there could be something left behind. This could be *very* big.

It could also be a chance for me to face my trauma head-on. I'd been having nightmares of that place. The rough rope chewing into my skin, the tranquil bubbling of the water filters inside the glowing aquariums, the biting stench of sweat and mold and chemicals. It made me sick to even think about. And I found that the more time passed, the worse my memories became. The aquariums weren't holding tropical fish; they were holding grotesque worms, fighting and eating each other in a mess of blood and organs. The chemicals weren't on a tray next to the table but instead being held over my body with intravenous bags, the acid and toxins slowly dripping directly into my veins.

Horrors multiplied and made the nightmares worse.

But if I faced it all head-on, with Gabriel at my side, then maybe the fear would loosen its grip?

I threw off the sheets and went over to my suitcase, pulling out a pair of black briefs and changing into those, leaving my boxers on the hotel floor.

"What are you doing?" Gabe asked, already tying his sneakers.

"I'm going with you." I hopped into a pair of black track pants, nearly falling over onto a skeptical-looking Gabriel.

His head cocked, arms crossed, Gabe says, "I think I'd rather you stay here."

"And miss out on this possible research for my next thriller novel? I don't think so."

He arched a bushy brow. I rolled my head and popped a couple of bones, sitting down on the edge of the bed. "I need to go, Gabe. All jokes aside, I feel like I have to see it again. With you there. While I feel safe. It's the only way I won't blow it up in my head. Besides, maybe I find something you don't."

He came over to me, crouching so that he balanced on the balls of his feet, his hands going to my knees. "Are you sure, Trist? I can FaceTime you when I get there. You don't have to go and relive it."

Those blue eyes swirled, like the crystal-clear waters of the Caribbean, inviting you to dive in headfirst. His touch was gentle, his hands warm against my skin. If it were my choice, we would stay locked up in this hotel room forever. High up above all our problems and worries. We'd spend the rest of our days naked and sweaty and dripping in passion, memorizing each dip and curve and line in each other's bodies. I'd write an endless amount of books, each one more inspired than the last, fed by the eternal presence of my muse.

"I need to go," I answered, determination in my voice keeping away any quivers that could give away how I really felt.

"Alright. If at any moment you feel like you need to leave, tell me, okay?"

"Okay."

His smile lit up his face, his lips coming to meet mine. His hands slipped higher up my legs. I savored the connection. We couldn't stay in this hotel room forever, but I could at least hold on to this moment for the rest of time, always remembering how warm and safe I felt kissing Gabe.

My boyfriend.

Hah. Who would have ever guessed?

Probably everyone who saw us interact for longer than two minutes.

We finished getting ready, conversation slowly dying out as the weight of this decision began settling on my shoulders. I had to sneak into the bathroom and run the water as I fought off a mini panic attack. A couple of cold splashes to the face did nothing for me, leading me to believe all those movie scenes were built on lies.

After a couple more minutes, I was able to pull it together, reminding myself that it was pure daylight and Gabriel would be at my side. There'd be no way that the Midnight Chemist was still somehow lurking in his hideout. They were likely far, far away from it, trying to lose themselves before they struck again.

The drive was somber, like we were driving to a funeral. We didn't really talk, and neither of us wanted to listen to music. Thoughts crashed around in my skull. I tried not to think about all the ways this could end up being a big mistake. I tried instead to focus on the trees that blurred past, the shops and the townhomes and the parks, all of them zipping away as we drove out of the city. Houses started to be more spread out, more run-down. Front yards full of trash and kid toys, cars that were rusted and missing wheels, dogs that needed at least three flea baths and a couple of good meals.

I could feel the hideout before we reached out, like a thick cape of dread was dropped over my head, instantly stifling me, making my breathing harder to control. Gabriel slowed down as the road gave way to dirt and gravel, leading up to a shack of a house, yellow crime scene tape still running around the perimeter like some fucked-up gift wrapping.

My stomach flipped. My mouth went ash dry. I squeezed my hands together as the car came to a stop. Things started to spin, the world itself, as if someone had plucked the earth between two fingers and slowly rolled it between them. I couldn't do this. It was a mistake. Too soon. Couldn't.

I was so close to death. I looked down and saw bright red blood around my wrists, pooling against my dark skin, dropping in puddles of rubies at my feet.

No. No, this was a massive fucking mistake, and the impending panic attack would be the price I had to pay for making it.

Fuck.

22

GABRIEL FERNANDEZ

I KNEW this would be a bad idea. It was too soon. Tristan still hadn't fully dealt with the trauma he'd experienced not even a week earlier, and now we were back to where it was all caused. I could see the fear and dread sink into him, his eyes wide as he looked out the car window at the beat-down shack. Yellow crime scene tape fluttered in the gentle breeze.

I turned the car back on. Tristan looked to me, head cocked.

"I'm taking you back," I said, already reversing the car down the gravel-filled driveway.

"Wait, no, hold up." Tristan put a hand on mine, closing it around me, his fingers touching the gearshift. "I need to do this."

"Trist, there's nothing you need to do in life except for sleep and taxes."

"And eating and drinking. And certain other things."

I narrowed my eyes. Guess he wasn't scared enough

to not be a smart-ass. I smirked, flipping my hand over so that his fingers locked with mine. His palm was warm against mine, his skin soft. The hands of a writer. Complete opposite to my calloused hand with much thicker fingers than his.

They fit perfectly together. "I'm being serious, Tristan. You don't have to do this if it's going to cause you more harm than good. I can take you back to the hotel. Or maybe Eric or Noah are doing something?"

"I don't need to be babysat," he said, looking back out the window. The house seemed to be mocking us, two windows on either side of the crooked door, one window cracked with a fluttering white curtain blowing in the wind. As if the damn thing were winking at us.

Come in, come in. I promise I won't bite.

I looked back to Tristan. It was a cloudy day today, the sun fighting its way through the thick gray wash. Somehow, even with the gloom, Tristan seemed to sparkle. I didn't want anything—or anyone—to dim that. "I just want to keep you safe, that's all."

"I'm safe when I'm by your side, Gabe." His hand squeezed mine. A blossoming kind of heat planted itself in my chest, its roots spreading outward. This was my boyfriend now. We were official. No more games, no more pretenses about keeping things professional.

I thought back to the last time Tristan wasn't at my side. He'd been taken that day. I nearly lost him. I never wanted that to happen again.

"If it gets to be too much, tell me, alright?"

He nodded. Fear still resided in his expression, in the

way his eyebrows crinkled together and his bottom lips slightly quivered. But there was also determination there. Maybe he really did need to do this. He'd be waking up in the middle of the night screaming bloody murder, saying the nightmares were so vivid... maybe being here could de-fang some of those nightmares.

It could also make them worse.

"Let's do this," he said, setting his sights directly ahead.

I switched the car back into drive and pulled ahead, stopping in another cloud of dust. This time, Tristan didn't think twice about pushing open the door and stepping out, the dust still settling.

"Hold on," I said, my hand going down to the concealed pistol I had brought with me. I wasn't leaving anything to chance today. "Let me go first."

"After you," Tristan said with a flourished bow. He wore that easy smile of his again. It made me like him even more, seeing how courageous and positive he could be in the face of such darkness. We were steps away from a place that could have easily been Tristan's gravesite, and yet he was smiling at me, his honey-warm brown eyes glittering even with the thick cloud that sat directly above us.

I took him in for a brief moment. He would be my pillar of strength. I always liked to think about pillars that held me up; it was how I got through the brutal years as a Marine. I thought about my best friend, I thought about my mom, I thought about myself. All three pillars kept me standing when bullets were flying and blood spraying.

Today, my pillar would be Tristan. Today and tomorrow and the day after and the day after that.

Taking the lead, I stepped in front of Tristan. The place had already been searched by the cops, but all they found for evidence were a few incomplete fingerprints, a mixture of toxic chemicals, and some strands of hair that didn't pull up any matches in the database.

Basically, they found nothing. Which didn't necessarily mean there was nothing inside.

The door, unlocked, opened on creaking hinges, slanting so that it scraped against the already scratched wooden floor. Like dented scars never meant to heal, never meant to scab over. The smell of wet and musty air hit me first. I went to turn on the lights, but nothing came on, so instead, I went for the drapes, opening each one. "Stick close to me," I said, going toward the first closed door. "I'm going to clear this place."

"I love it when you talk dirty," Tristan teased behind me. I smirked before throwing open the door, revealing a dirty (and empty) bedroom. There was a mattress with no bed frame sitting on the floor, the bedsheets having been torn off and processed into evidence already. Fingerprint dust still clung to the dingy bedside table. A tiny window was boarded up with thin planks of wood, making this room darker than the living room.

I went to the next door and the next. Each room was empty, our footsteps seeming to echo as if we had entered into a cavernous expanse. The house was quiet.

"How are you feeling?" I asked Tristan as we reached the entrance to the basement.

"A little light-headed. But fine."

I looked into his eyes, trying to spot any kind of sign to turn around.

It was all I saw. Everything screamed at me to push him right back through the front door and get him in the car, far from this literal hellhole we were about to climb down into.

But I had to trust him. Wasn't that what created the foundation for a solid relationship?

The door to the basement opened with a loud yawn, the wood hitting the floor with a clatter. I went down first, Tristan's hand falling between my shoulders as he followed. I didn't want to pull out my gun and worry Tristan any more than he already was, but my hand did hover over it, ready for anything.

The basement itself had been mostly emptied. There was nothing, or no one, to be ready for. The aquariums were gone, the tables that held them still there, covered in a dark black tablecloth. The restraints that had tied Tristan down were also gone, along with the tray of chemicals and used syringes next to it. It smelled clean, too. Like Pine-Sol, as if the police had cleaned the place up after they left.

Or maybe it wasn't the police? They weren't exactly known for their homely manners.

"Fuck, this is weird." Tristan stood with his hands in the pocket of his jeans. He wore a pearl necklace inter-mittently set with sapphires—something he'd spotted in an Instagram ad and mentioned he wanted. I liked surprises, so I'd ordered it the second he wasn't looking at my phone. He went to fiddle with one of the bright blue balls.

"Looks like the cops took everything," I said, scanning the small space. I went to the tables and lifted the cloth, seeing only dirt and dust bunnies. "Nothing."

I didn't want to prolong this. I could come back later in the day and do a more thorough search, but for now, this would have to be enough.

"Come on. Let's go get some lunch and walk Piedmont."

I started toward the steps when Tristan grabbed my elbow.

"Wait... while I was here, I remember hearing something. It sounded like a door. A heavy door, not like the one that leads into the basement." Tristan looked around, doing a spin. He moved to the center of the room. There, he stood with his eyes closed, the wrinkles on his forehead multiplying. I didn't even breathe. I watched him as the memory slowly started to resurface. "It sounded like it had come from this direction."

Tristan took a few steps forward, toward the wall. The table that held the row of aquariums was now missing its aquatic inhabitants. The thin black drape hung down to the floor, pooling by Tristan's feet. He cocked his head, stretched out his hand, fingers running over the smooth brick.

"Wait a second..." Tristan leaned forward. "Look at this."

I went over to his side, leaned over the table. Tristan's finger traced a clear line in the brick, one that I had completely missed. I followed it up, to the left, back down, disappearing behind the table.

"Holy fuck," I said. "Help me with this."

Tristan grabbed one end of the table, and I grabbed the other. We moved it to the center of the room and went back to the wall. The seam was so obvious to me now. How the hell did I miss it?

"You're good, Trist." I grabbed his face in my hands and kissed him. Hard. "Just don't come for my job, alright?"

He gave me a wink and a cocky grin. "Maybe we can open up our own agency together. Sherlock and Watson, except we're a fanfic where they fuck. A lot."

I kissed him again. Couldn't help it. "I like that plan," I said, turning back to the hidden door. I put a hand on the brick that looked the most worn-out, likely out of years of use. It moved, inches at first, until something gave way and the entire chunk of brick wall opened up wide, revealing a glowing purple and blue room behind it.

The glow came from two massive aquariums, much larger than any of the ones that had been in the previous room. The water was crystal clear, and clown fish of all types swam inside them, drifting in and out of a bed of bright anemones glowing a neon blue and red under the aquarium lights. There were potted plants that had timed lamps attached to them, thriving up toward the ground, as if knowing the sun was only a couple of feet away. There was a small cot with a stack of books next to it. I recognized the topmost book: *Twisting Razors*. The same book we were reading in Tristan's book club.

At least the Midnight Chemist had good taste in books, if not a little too on the nose.

"This is... insane." Tristan looked around the room, the blue and purple glow bouncing off his pearl necklace.

"It's a hideout inside of a hideout. I can't believe the cops missed this." I looked to Tristan, appreciative of him facing his fears to be here. "And without you, I might have missed it, too."

"You would have found it," Tristan said with a dismissive wave. He went to a shelf, the clear case containing a row of clearly labeled vials.

Actinostephanus haeckeli.

Phyllodiscus semoni.

T. stephensoni.

A quick Google search revealed what we were looking at. "These are some of the most toxic sea anemone species in existence," I said, looking back at the tanks containing what now appeared to be a farm of powerful venom. They seemed harmless, like a rainbow-colored garden—only underwater. But I remember learning quickly after my Jungle Warfare training anything bright and colorful was likely lethal as all hell. The unnatural colors were supposed to serve as a warning.

I opened the glass case and picked out a vial. "There's a lot number," I said, tilting over the vial of milky liquid. "Maybe these weren't bought that long ago."

Tristan nodded, smiling. "It could be how we find this fucker."

"Possibly." I took a photo of the vial, along with the rest of the neatly organized shelf. It was cooler inside the case, too. I noticed a vent behind the vials that must have worked to regulate the temperature.

Whoever built this knew what they were doing.

I crouched down and opened a drawer. There were more empty vials, along with some syringes and gloves. Curiously, next to those items was a neatly organized makeup section. Nothing too elaborate, but there were a couple of items that caught my attention. A foundation for someone with a lighter complexion told me more about how this person looked, along with a brush that must have had some sort of DNA trace on it. There was ChapStick and lotion and some other skin care things but nothing of note.

The next drawer had an even more interesting find: cell phones. Quite a few of them. Mostly older-model iPhones but a couple of others thrown in as well. And they were all labeled with the same neat handwriting that had written the labels on the vials.

Names. Familiar names. Ones I had burned into my memory after hours and hours of digging through the lives of each name.

All of these were victims of the Midnight Chemist. He had kept their phones. That wasn't something even the cops had revealed—or maybe they didn't even know.

One of the phones didn't have a label. I found that to be a little odd. Why were all the rest clearly marked and this one was set to the side without any way to tell whose it was? It was a newer iPhone, too, different from the ones that didn't even have tracking yet.

I grabbed the unlabeled phone. I held the power button down, but the screen stayed dead. It needed a charge.

"Who do you think that belongs to?" Tristan asked, looking down at the phone.

"We're going to find out." I looked around, wondering if there were any other hidden clues. I was starting to see the full picture, but there were pieces missing. We weren't at the finish line yet.

"Let's see if—" *BANG*.

We froze, solidifying into a pair of breathing statues. I broke the icy spell first, yanking my gun out from the holster and aiming it out toward the rest of the basement.

That was the trapdoor that led down here. Someone had slammed it shut.

A loud *zap* sound followed the bang and then a quick flicker as the lights all turned off in unison, the power having been turned off, plunging us into a sudden and all-consuming night.

23

TRISTAN HALL

I FUMBLED FOR MY PHONE, digging into my pocket and yanking it out, my hand shaking as I hit the flashlight button.

"You had a gun this entire time?" I asked in a shocked whisper.

"Shh."

The flashlight bounced off the glass aquariums, creating a horrifying display of shadow puppets that seemed to be taunting us from their invisible stages. This was worst-case scenario. We were in the belly of the beast, and the beast just snapped its jaws shut around us. I wanted to curl up in a corner and accept my fate, but then I remembered I had made it out of this once; I could do it again.

"Keep behind me," Gabe said, inching toward the stairs. "And try to aim the light wherever I aim my gun."

It was difficult at first. He would look left, and my light would still be aimed to the right. Fear pooled in the back of my throat, like spoiled milk fighting its way to come back up. I tried to reframe this situation: use it as research. I could write a killer thriller when all this was done.

The caveat being that I had to survive this in order to write it.

Gabriel put an arm out and came to a sudden stop. We were right in front of the stairs that led up to the rest of the house. Sure enough, the door we had come in from was now shut, only a small slice of light breaking through. I could hear my own heartbeat. Or was that Gabriel's? I couldn't tell.

He started moving forward again. It felt like I had swallowed a gallon of sand, my mouth as dry as ash. I swallowed, but it hurt, nearly making me cough. I put a fist up against my mouth to cover any noise as we slowly went up the steps, the thin wood planks creaking even as we inched upward. Gabriel had the gun aimed up toward the door.

He reached out, his hand holding one of the handles. I took a breath and steadied myself. I had no idea what was on the other side of that door, except I did know it was our only way out. The darkness felt like a living thing, its inky black tentacles stretching up from the basement and trying to close around my ankles, dragging me back down into the depths. A cockroach scuttled up the wall near my head.

Gabriel pushed the door open and exploded outward, practically leaping out of the floor, gun aimed. I held my breath. I expected a shot, something to say it was all over, that Gabe had ended the nightmare.

Instead, I heard Gabriel call back to me. "No one's here. You can come out."

I hurried up the last few steps, the wood bending under my weight. The air was still musty and wet, but I took a big gulp of it, filling my lungs. The lights were off up here as well, but there was plenty of sunlight coming in through the cracked window, allowing me to turn off my phone.

"Hurry, let's get out of here," Gabriel said. He was clicked fully into bodyguard mode, his posture at high alert, his muscles twitching as he continually scanned the room through the sight of his gun. If I wasn't so scared, I'd probably be turned on.

I stuck close to Gabe, a hand on his shoulder as he led me through the shack and back out, back to safety. The air tasted much better out here. I let go of a breath I hadn't realized I was holding, replacing it with another big chug of oxygen. The sun on my skin felt like being kissed by God herself. I half wanted to drop to my knees and kiss the ground but figured that would be way too dramatic.

We hurried to the car instead. I jumped into the passenger seat, Gabe having reholstered his gun as he climbed into the driver's seat. He gave the property one last scan before reversing, the crooked grin of the broken door seeming to taunt us as we left.

"Holy shit," I said, another exhale coming out with a shocked laugh attached. "Think that was the

Midnight Chemist back there? Maybe it was the wind?"

Gabe shook his head. He gripped the wheel with one hand, his forearm pushing at the fabric of his rolled-up sleeve. "I think it was the Chemist. Those fish look taken care of. He might have been coming back. Probably heard us and freaked out, ran, and slammed the door shut."

"And cut the power? Maybe to slow us down?"

"Probably." Gabe looked over at me and winked. "Nice deduction, Watson."

I chuckled. The further we put that house behind us, the better I began to feel. I lowered the window and let the wind rush in, sticking my arm out and letting my hand get carried in the invisible currents.

And then I remembered. "The phone. Do you still have it?"

"I do. It's in my pocket." He shifted so I could reach in and grab it.

"Do you have a car charger?" I asked, flipping the phone over and seeing that the port was one of the newer ones.

He slowed down at a red light and reached across me, grabbing a long white cable from inside the glove compartment. "Would this work?"

I checked the ends. "Yup," I said, plugging it into the dead phone. It only took about a minute for the screen to blink on, the white Apple logo sitting in the center. It opened straight into an icon-littered homepage.

"Yes," I said, pumping my fist. "No password."

I went straight to the settings option and clicked on

"My Phone." It gave me a screen full of information: how much storage was in the phone, what version it was, what model, and—most importantly—who it belonged to.

"Mason Martinez," I said out loud. "That's who owned this phone."

"Holy shit." Gabe nearly slammed on the brakes. "That was Grayson's boyfriend—one of the Chemist's most recent victims."

I looked over at him, my deduction skills only taking me so far.

"Is... was Grayson's boyfriend the killer?"

Gabe made a sudden turn, taking us onto the highway. I raised the window, the screech of the wind becoming too loud. "I don't know. I do know that I want to talk to him now. He's a bartender at the Mandarin Hotel."

I played with a smooth pearl on my necklace. This felt big. Monumental. Shit was starting to shift. I just couldn't tell if it was shifting in my direction or not. Could the Chemist be leading us off the trail or directly onto it?

There was only one way to find out. "I'm coming with you," I said, just in case that hadn't already been known.

"Of course," Gabe said, his eyes on the road and a smirk playing on his face. "Sherlock needs his Watson."

My literary heart fluttered at the continual comparison. As scared as I'd been in that dark basement, I realized that I'd never actually feared for my life. Not in the way I had when I was blindfolded and strapped down to a table. I had tasted death then. Felt it creep into my body, ready to sever me from whatever corporeal form I had.

But with Gabriel there, I had felt safe. Scared as fuck, yeah, but safe, too.

I looked out the window at the blur of office buildings as we drove past downtown Atlanta. I had no idea what was ahead, but I felt confident I could face it now that I had Mr. Holmes at my side.

———

THE MANDARIN WAS a bougie affair full of suited bellhops and overly attendant hotel staff that all complemented the glossy veneer. Money dripped from every detail, like the crystals that cascaded from the picturesque chandeliers that lit the lobby. They hung above a beautiful display of cranes sculpted out of shining glass, their long necks and spread wings appearing to be caught in midflight. I sat in one of the green velvet chairs as Gabriel spoke to the front desk, asking where their bar was located. While he did that, I decided to dig through the phone a little bit more.

There weren't that many text messages, but there was an app that interested me. It was next to the black-and-yellow Grindr icon—blue with a cartoon flame on it. It was called Burner, an app meant to create fake numbers. Commonly used by cheaters and drug dealers.

The openly displayed Grindr icon told me he wasn't all that concerned about hiding his collection of dick pics, so I leaned more toward the "drug dealer" side of the scale.

Gabriel came back with the directions to the bar. I followed him to the elevator bay, explaining what I had found.

"Can we see any messages or calls he made on that app?"

I shook my head. "They get erased after a forty-eight-hour period. Nothing's there." We entered the elevator and rode it up to the twelfth floor. We stepped out into a bright waiting area, decked out in vibrant golden wallpaper, the ivy-green carpet leading up to a smiling hostess.

"Bar Margo?" Gabe asked.

"Yes, sir. Are you two dining at a table, or would you like bar seating?"

"We're okay with the bar," he answered. She motioned into the busy restaurant, tables full of people having an early dinner, spread out around the circular bar that took up the center of the room. It was made of smooth gray-and-black marble, an impressive display of liquors from all over the world perfectly placed and displayed on a central column of the same marble.

I looked at the bartenders, moving behind the bar like a choreographed dance troupe, dressed in all black with hair tied back or cut short. Some tossed shakers over their heads, and others swirled cards between their fingers as they closed out tabs.

One of them was somehow involved with the Midnight Chemist. I had to prepare myself for the possibility that one of them *was* the Midnight Chemist. They would instantly recognize me, but I had no idea what they looked like.

A shiver flew down my spine. Gabriel grabbed my hand in his and walked us to an open spot at the bar, where we sat on two scarlet-red stools. A golden dragon hung above the bar, holding glowing orbs in its claws that washed the space in a warm light.

"What can I get you two?" It was a tattooed bartender with long blonde hair.

"We're looking for Mason. We heard he works here?"

"Sure, let me grab him for you." She went around to the other side of the bar, the view obstructed by the column of expensive bottles.

It took a couple of agonizing minutes before the tattooed bartender reappeared, but Mason still wasn't anywhere in sight. Had he gotten wind that a detective was looking for him? Could he have bolted before we could even question him?

I shot Gabriel an anxious look, but the guy looked cool as an iced-over hell. I knew he had to be boiling inside, but his exterior didn't give anything away, his big lips set in a relaxed smile, his hands casually bunched into a fist and resting on the bar. Unlike mine, which were currently pinned under both of my bouncing legs.

Another bartender appeared shortly after. The tattooed one pointed at us. Mason looked our way, an icy glare locking with mine. He bundled up a white towel and tossed it under the bar before walking toward us with a stride that belonged on a runway somewhere in Paris. He had the look, too, not just the walk. Tall and perfectly proportioned, his long legs and lean frame made to wear some high-fashion design. He had short dark black hair, a silver ring catching the light and bouncing it off his eyebrow, near where a scar slashed through and left a bare patch of darker skin.

If he was the Midnight Chemist, then he didn't seem very shaken to see me sitting there. He just seemed... suspicious.

"Kass was saying you needed me?" He leaned against the bar with his hip, eyes sizing us both up.

"We do. Is there somewhere quieter we can speak?" Gabe asked. The bar wasn't too loud, but I think he was more concerned about someone listening to us.

"Here's fine."

"Right," Gabe said. He had run directly into a brick wall. Gabe had looked into him, he told me everything he found on him. I stared at Mason, tried reading him like one of the books I would write, making a character summary of him: mid-twenties, dark and broody, sunflowers and penguins always make him smile. Had a rough start to life but was making a good life for himself now, working through getting a college degree. Gabe mentioned that his social media presence did seem to taper off over the last couple of years, with his most recent photo just a blurry shot of some food he took five months ago. Still, that wasn't entirely odd. Plenty of people stopped using their social media.

But where did being a serial killer fit into any of that?

"We came to ask you some questions. I'm Detective

Gabriel Fernandez with Stonewall Investigations, and this is Tristan, my associate."

Nice. Vague enough to mean anything.

Mason's nostrils flared. He started to shift backward. Was that fear in his blown out pupils? "I don't speak to the cops."

"We're not cops," Gabriel said. "I work on my own."

"Didn't you just say he's your associate?" Mason pointed at me.

"Still not cops," I reiterated and sat up a little straighter. He had sharp green eyes, and they seemed to try to be figuring me out.

"What is this about?"

"The Midnight Chemist," Gabe said. I could see an immediate shift in Mason's demeanor. His pupils exploded, his hands fisted. A vein in his forehead throbbed against his tan skin. "We found your phone, along with the phones of all his past victims. How'd your phone get there, Mason?"

He blinked, searched for words. He reached for his phone, but Gabriel took it back. "How'd it get there?"

Mason's sharp eyes were dulled now. Shaken. "I'm—I —fuck. Let's go to the courtyard. Kass, watch my spot for me?"

"You got it," she said, rubbing his shoulder as Mason walked out through a gap in the bar. He didn't even look back to see if we followed him, winding through the packed tables and into a dim hallway, toward a heavy red door. He pushed it open with a shoulder, sunlight pouring in. Outside was a small and mostly empty courtyard, the bubbling sound of a fountain mixing with the chirping birds that flitted between the trees. The hotel towered up toward the slightly cloudy sky, a small path leading out toward the street.

"Where was my phone?" Mason asked as we sat at an empty table.

"It was found somewhere we know the Midnight Chemist had been," Gabriel said. I could tell he didn't want to give out any unnecessary details. "So it is yours?"

"It's mine." He swallowed and rubbed at his face. "Please. I think I still have voicemails on there. I need to hear them."

I cocked my head. Voicemails? Gabriel looked hesitant, but Mason was close to tears. "Is this about Grayson?" I asked, immediately connecting the emotional dots.

He nodded. "I saved his voicemails after he died. Then I lost my phone and felt like I lost him all over again."

"How did you lose it?" Gabriel asked, still holding on to the phone.

His next words nearly knocked me out of my chair. "I think it happened the night I slept with the Midnight Chemist."

24

GABRIEL FERNANDEZ

I KEPT the surprise from appearing on my face as Mason described to us the night he met up with the Midnight Chemist.

"Grayson and I are—were—open," he started off, stopping to chew on a nail. "I was talking to this guy off Grindr. His account name was fish something. I can't really remember it—I blocked him after that night so he never showed back up on my grid."

"Do you mind if I record this conversation?" I asked.

Mason narrowed his eyes. He looked down at my phone, now on the center of the small round table. "I don't know if I'm good with that, actually."

"It's okay," I said, grabbing my phone back. "Would you feel better if Tristan and I just took some notes?"

Mason took a deep breath. His eyes darted around the courtyard. He was clearly nervous about something, and it didn't seem to be just about the Chemist.

I had to be careful here. Mason clearly had information, but he didn't seem all that willing to give it up. I had to be sure I didn't spook him. Had to reassure him somehow that we were on his side.

For now.

"Here," I said, taking out his phone and placing it on the same spot mine had been. "We'll give this back to you. Just tell us everything you know."

His eyes jumped from me to Tristan to the phone. He reached for the phone, and this time, I didn't snatch it away from him. He clutched it in both hands, looking off at the fountain. The sun broke through some clouds and made something shimmer in the corner of Mason's eye. I thought it might have been makeup at first—he wore some, judging by his perfect complexion and extra-long lashes—but realized it was a tear.

"I thought I'd never hear him again," he said, sniffing as he pocketed the phone. "Thank you."

I nodded, as did Tristan. I had to trust that this trade-off wouldn't come back to bite me in the ass somehow.

"Did you get to see him? The Chemist?" Tristan asked, leaning forward.

Mason nodded. I honed in on him like a hawk locking onto a rodent. "What did he look like?"

"It was dark in his house," Mason said. "And I was really drunk. I Ubered there after the club. Grayson was supposed to come with me but got caught up eating pizza with our friends. He told me to go and have fun, that he'd be there when I got home... so I did."

"Where did you two meet?"

"A hotel. He said he was visiting."

"Which hotel?" Tristan asked.

"The Juniper, in Mid—"

"Town," Tristan said and looked to me. Fear bloomed in his eyes, like a rotting rose.

That was the hotel we were staying at.

I put a hand on Tristan's leg and squeezed. Mason's eyes darted down at the touch. Instead of bristling, he seemed to relax a bit, shoulders shifting so that they were less tense. Unlike Tristan, who now sat like there was a steel rod rammed down his back.

I wanted to comfort him more, but there was still a job to do. I turned my attention back to Mason. "Do you remember what day? And time?"

"I already asked who was staying in that room. The hotel gave me some fake name. Couldn't find it anywhere."

"What was the name?" I asked.

"Marlin Brooks."

I wrote that down into the Notes app on my phone as Mason continued. He described the incense Marlin had lit and the offer of drugs or alcohol before they hooked up. "I told him no thanks, and we took off our pants. He was tall and skinny. White, with medium-ish dark hair. I don't even know what color his eyes are... I do remember seeing something as I was leaving, though. I think the sweat must have taken off some of his makeup.

"I noticed a birthmark on his face. It looked weirdly like a fish. Not an anatomically correct fish or anything, but like those simple fish you draw with one line in a notebook."

That would explain the concealer and foundation we found in the hideout. "Why didn't you go to the police with any of this?"

"Because I can't have them looking my way... I just can't. I'm here, supporting my mom and my little sister. If they dug around too much, then—" He shook his head and held the phone to his chest. "I wanted to. Trust me. I made it out that night by some kind of grace. But then Grayson went to see him, a week later. I was out of town. I got the call when I was about to board my flight back home; Grayson was dead, found left in a ditch and pumped up with chemicals." He choked back tears.

Unfortunately, though, we weren't here to help him process his trauma. We were here for information, and I felt like we were getting closer and closer to something that could crack this case. I had to push forward.

"Did Grayson mention anything about this man to you? Anything they spoke about before they met up?"

Mason shook his head. He rubbed at this throat. Looked at his watch. "Nothing. Listen, I have to get back to work. I told you all I know." He started to stand, the wrought-iron chair scratching against the brick floor. "If I think of anything, I'll call you."

I was going to stop him but figured it would do more harm than good. At least this line of communication was open now.

"Mason, please stay safe. The Midnight Chemist is still out there," I said.

"I will... And thanks for this," he said, holding up the phone before slipping it back into the pocket of his black pants. He went back inside the hotel, leaving Tristan and me alone in the courtyard. A line of traffic honked loudly from the street, cutting off Tristan's "holy shit."

"That went well," I said, turning to him so that our knees touched. I loved when our bodies connected, no matter in what way. Could be a hand on the shoulder, a knee against a knee, a bump with the backs of our hands. No matter what it was, so long as Tristan's body touched mine, I could feel sparks fly. It wasn't something I was really used to. Being physical with someone always meant things were leading toward sex. But with Tristan, touch was about so much more.

It felt like every brush, every subtle stroke, every tiny nudge was another drop of water onto our garden, vibrant red roses opening their thick and velvety petals whenever our bodies connected.

It was magical. I just wished I could enjoy it without the heavy cloud that hung above us since the start of our relationship.

"Think we got enough?" Tristan asked.

"I think we got what we needed." I rose, Tristan following. His elbow brushed mine—sparks. "I'm going to speak to the hotel and see if I can get any surveillance footage from the day Mason was there. We've got a decent description with an identifying feature, and we know how to contact Mason now."

"I can't believe he stayed at the same hotel we're in. Jesus Christ." Tristan gave a self-deprecating laugh, like wind being sucked out of a balloon. "What are the odds?"

"Not sure. I was never big into gambling. Or math."

"Good, me either. Guess that's why I stuck to working with words instead." Tristan scratched at the back of his neck, the wings on his forearm tattoo flexing with his arm. "We can't stay there. Not anymore."

"That's fine. I can look into other hotels."

Tristan shook his head, hand falling on my wrist. More sparks. Fiery and bright, shooting up and down the entire length of my body. "No, no more hotels. I want to start getting things back to normal, and that means no more housekeeping."

"I was just getting used to it, too." I slanted my grin, cocked my head, stole a kiss.

Fireworks.

"How about I stay over your place and pay you back by making the bed, then?" Tristan's smile was wide. It was just us in the courtyard, but looking down into those warm brown eyes made it feel like the entire world was emptied out except for us. He was perfection, in every sense of the word. How the hell had I been able to resist the pull I felt toward him from the second we met? The circumstances were complete and utter shit, but the result of us meeting was turning out to be beauty shining through the chaos.

"I can think of a couple other ways you can repay me," I said, teasing Tristan with a nibble on his lower lip. Having him stay over my place was exactly what I wanted. It wasn't as impenetrable as the hotel, but I'd installed a new security system that kept watch over the entire property, not just the front door. I also put in a fence crowned with sharp iron peaks that made it impossible to climb. I didn't care that I was slowly turning my house into a fortress. It gave me a greater peace of mind knowing that Tristan would be safe, and that's all that mattered, aesthetics and landscaping be damned.

"Come," I said, my stomach rumbling. "Let's get some lunch and talk about things that don't have to do with the case. It's been a long few days."

"It sure fucking has," Tristan said, leaning into me as we walked into the Mandarin Hotel, slipping back into its dark hallways and red satin walls. We decided to treat ourselves and have lunch there, where we sat in a booth underneath a plume of peacock feathers placed in the center of a golden frame.

I flexed my neck as I looked over the menu. "God, I could use a good massage."

"I've been told I have golden hands," Tristan smirked at me from across the table. His dark red polo shirt was nearly the exact same shade of red as the booth we sat in.

"Then maybe that's how you can pay for your room and board," I shot back before stretching my legs out under the table. I found his, resting my ankle against him. "Start with the knots in my shoulder."

"And work my way down?"

"Exactly," I said, hooking my foot against his leg. He cocked his head, brown eyes searching mine. He was so fucking handsome, with his short dark hair that was starting to grow back after a recent haircut, the top curls coming out tight, shining under the golden lighting of the hotel restaurant. I loved waking up to him nestled into me, that soft head of hair tickling my chin. I'd wake him up with kisses, which would slowly (and sometimes quickly) evolve into much more.

Things changed since we had made us official. There was no more beating around the bush, no more testing the temperature between us. It was now full throttle, like someone had slammed down on the gas and launched us forward. We fucked without reservations, giving it all to each other, letting the other take what they wanted. It was beautiful and primal and so fucking blissful.

As we looked through the menus and made our orders, still playing footsie with each other under the table, even as the waiter joked with us about the catch of the day, I realized then that I had found my one. He checked off all the boxes for me and made me happy in a way that I could barely even comprehend.

I realized then that I would do anything to keep him safe.

I'd die for him if I had to. No doubt about it.

25

TRISTAN HALL

STAYING BACK at Gabe's wasn't as scary as I'd made it out to be in my head. Admittedly, the first couple of nights were pretty difficult. I felt like a kid again, but I had to ask Gabriel to leave the light on for the first night. He didn't even think twice about it, getting up from the bed and flicking it on before climbing back in, his arms forming a cave I could escape into and feel safe in.

It was nice. Beyond nice. It felt like I was slowly crawling out of my own grave. I had been so close to giving up, losing the spark and just turning into a monotonous robot. But Gabriel came into my life and changed all that. I was *excited* about life for once. It reflected in my work, my diet, my exercise.

I wanted to thank him somehow. Nothing I could do would really encompass how grateful I was that Gabe was mine, but I had to at least try. That's why, as he was showering and getting ready for tonight's book club, I went out to the front and grabbed the Amazon order I had gotten delivered, dragging it into the garage and hiding the box behind a dusty corner.

With the box hidden, I went back into the house, going to the steam-filled bathroom, where Gabe was toweling himself off. All six feet and three inches of himself, dripping and shining under the white vanity lights. I shook my head, unable to comprehend how the hell I'd landed such a hot hunk of a man.

"You ready?" he asked casually as he dried off his hair, his heavy cock swinging between his legs, crowned by a dark bush.

I was instantly hard. If we weren't already running fifteen minutes late, I would have dropped to my knees and sucked the water droplets right off his thick cock.

Instead, I exhibited some self-control and went to brush my teeth instead. "Ready when you are," I said, watching Gabe's bare ass jiggle its way out of the bathroom. He came back dressed in khaki shorts and a black V-neck T-shirt. I glanced down, smiled.

"Are you not wearing any underwear?" I asked, noticing the bulge.

"Is it that obvious?"

"A little bit," I said. I reached out and grabbed a handful, kissing him with my minty breath. "Stay like that. It'll make things easier for when we get back home."

He chuckled and wiggled his crotch in my grip as he kissed me back.

We somehow managed to finish getting ready without getting dickstracted. Five minutes later and we were in the car, heading toward Jake and Noah's new house. Now that the two were finding a groove together, they'd decided to pull another big trigger and get a mortgage together.

Their new house was in Decatur, a tree-covered neighborhood with a mix of modest homes that were very obviously flipped to large mansions with huge front yards and expensive cars lining the cobblestone driveways.

Jake and Noah lived in neither, having bought a recently renovated home from the 1950s, complete with oddly angled windows and a stretched-out garage that looked ready to dock a spaceship. The exterior sported a fresh coat of paint, black with slate-gray trim, a bright blue door drawing the eye. We walked past a row of lavender bushes and stepped onto the porch. The sounds of our friends already inside drifted through the open windows. I could hear Jess's high-pitched laugh and Eric's gravelly voice.

I rang the doorbell and was soon greeted by a smiling Noah, looking good in a pair of black pants and a bright blue shirt, a small pink whale winking at me from the chest pocket.

"Noah, are you kidding me right now? This place is beautiful, man." I gave him a tight hug and stepped inside, smelling a mix of cleaning products and fresh roses, likely coming from the big red candles flickering above the fireplace.

"You haven't even gotten the full tour yet. Come," Noah said, waving us in as he walked us through the house. We greeted the gang, who were gathered in the sunken living room, sitting around a buffet of snacks:

cheeses and olives and almonds, sitting around a bucket of icy-cold champagne, wine, and beer. Noah then took us through all the rooms, showing us the one he was most proud of: the library. It doubled as Noah's office, now that he worked from home half of the week. It was a cozy space, the walls covered in beautiful rich green wallpaper. There were four connected bookcases, all of them looking like they were pulled right out of a time machine, with clawed legs and ancient-looking wood, the trim intricately detailed with swoops and curves as if it were made of clay. Each shelf was packed to the brim with books, spines facing outward in a colorful display of stories.

Noah led us back to the living room, where Colton had center stage, telling the group about a harrowing incident he had at the grocery store today.

"And then the cart just rolls downhill, straight toward the back of a Bentley. Do I look like I have Bentley money?"

Eric laughed and rubbed Colton's leg. "Yes. Yes, you do."

The rest of the group broke out into laughter as Colton blushed. We took our seats, Gabe grabbing a beer and handing me one. I glanced at him as he sat cross-legged next to Noah. He was about twice Noah's size, like a gorilla sitting next to a chimp. And still, he looked like he fit in perfectly. He wasn't just my bodyguard or private detective anymore; Gabe had become part of the group, as easily as if he'd been with us from the start.

And it wasn't just Gabe, either. Our group had started off with just Noah, Eric, and me, figuring things out as we went. Now our family had grown exponentially, all of us gathered together so we could talk books, get drunk, and have a good time.

Well, almost all of us. "Where's Evan?" I asked Yvette.

She took a big sip out of her wineglass and said, "He's gone."

"Where'd he go?" Tia asked, leaning forward so she was perched on the edge of the couch. Yvette sat next to her on a leather love seat.

"I don't know," Yvette said with a shrug. "We broke up."

Jess made a soap-opera-like gasp. "Seriously?"

"Mhmm."

Steven, who sat next to me on the couch, leaned forward to grab a bottle of wine, holding my knee for stability. "He gave me weird vibes anyway," he said as he poured himself another glass.

"Same, if I'm being honest," Noah said. "You can do so much better, girl."

"I have to agree with him," Jake said. I doubted it was on purpose, but he and Noah were matching in dark green shirts and khaki shorts.

"Did you do it?" Tia asked.

Yvette gave a nod. "Honestly, he was starting to say some off-color things. I think he got caught up in one of those online 4chan groups. I wanted to cut things off before we got any more serious."

"Good call," Eric said, Colton nodding his head in agreement.

I wasn't all that surprised, either. Relieved, actually. Yvette was a boss-ass woman. She had an established career, a great family, and was a solid friend. I'd met her when we were in college, and she slid into the group like the last wheel we needed to take off. Noah, Eric, Yvette, and I became a little family unit, spending days studying together, eating, partying, and just hanging out. I wanted her to find someone who only enhanced those shining aspects about her, not dimmed them.

Gabe's leg fell against mine, his knee on mine.

I wanted her to find someone like Gabriel. A man who wasn't only a knight in shining armor but who was the king, too, and the jester and the court and the castle. He encompassed it all. Safety and warmth and sex and laughter and love.

It was all there. God damn. I got lucky with this one.

Steven bumped his shoulder into me as he reached for some grapes. He leaned in and apologized. Maybe he and Yvette could spark something? I vaguely remembered him mentioning he was bi, and they always had some good conversations together, usually breaking off into a corner after the book club to talk about philosophy.

"But whatever, enough about me. Let's get to the book. Jake, Noah, you guys take it away." Yvette dipped her head and flourished her arms before grabbing the book at her side, a rainbow assortment of sticky notes and tabs sticking out from the pages.

"Alright," Noah said with a clap of his hands. They were hosting tonight's meeting, so they had to come up with whatever drinking game we would play. "Tonight, it's all about *friendship*. The book focuses a lot on the friend group, and I love ours, so why not celebrate that? Every time someone brings up an old memory or inside joke tonight, we *all* drink. Sound good?"

The room broke into nods and approvals. Gabe shifted next to me, his leg pressing against mine. I realized then that we'd never really made an official announcement about our new relationship status. I told Eric about it when I last saw him, but the rest of the group didn't know yet.

Or rather, they knew but just didn't say anything. Not like Gabe and I were trying very hard to hide it. I practically sat on his lap, and his hand was resting against mine, fingers lazily playing with each other. I noticed Tia throw a few curious glances our way, her grin tipping over into a full-blown smile. Maybe once we were done with tonight's book club, I'd bring it up. Or maybe I just didn't have to? That's what was so magical about this group of friends—no, family—that we had formed over the years. There was a general sense of unwavering support and love between us, for whatever it was we ended up doing. We didn't have to feel judged or worried, nor did we ever have to make big announcements about life changes. Our bonds were stone solid, the foundation of our friendships just as strong.

"Let's jump into *Twisting Razors*," Noah said, opening his book with a flair. I took the cue and opened mine. Admittedly, the last couple of chapters had gone unread.

Who would have thought reading about a serial killer

while currently being targeted by one wouldn't exactly be an enjoyable experience?

Jake cleared his throat and kicked things off. "Did anyone else notice how Kenneth, our main character, continues to see that weird fox in the neighborhood? I'm wondering, and bear with me here, guys, but is that a sign he's hallucinating all of this?" Jake asked. He had one leg crossed over the other, a bright yellow highlighter against the corner of his mouth.

I had to admit the thought had crossed my mind. But the fox also might have another meaning. My mind worked well with metaphors and symbolism. "What if it keeps showing up because foxes are sly and cunning? What if it's trying to tell us that Kenneth is the killer?"

The room got quiet as they all started to process the bomb I just dropped.

"I thought the same thing," Tia echoed. "I told y'all that's what was happening from the start."

"She did," Jess said, supporting her girl.

Steven broke the silence first. "You know, that's actually kind of a genius idea." He smiled and squeezed my leg.

"I mean, if the author of the group didn't pick up on the twist, then I think there'd be a problem," I said with a chuckle.

"That would explain why he seems to always be around when there's been a murder," Colton said. He looked down at the book on his lap as if he were seeing it for the first time. "I thought it was because Kenneth was a target, but what if you're right—what if he's the one behind it all?"

Steven shook his head, rubbed the back of his neck. He wore a long-sleeved orange T-shirt with thick white stripes outlined in thin black, his leg bouncing so that it shook the couch we were crammed into. "No, I think that might be too obvious, actually."

Gabriel leaned over me and looked at Steven with surprise. "How's that obvious?"

"It just *feels* obvious. I always like to dig a little deeper. I don't think it's Kenneth. I think it's his best friend, Nicki. I think she has some kind of obsession with him, and she's taking out all the people he loves, one by one. Until he's only left with her."

I cocked my head. The puzzle I had arranged in my head broke apart, the pieces shuffling in new directions, fitting in ways I hadn't noticed before. Steven's theory sounded plausible, and he went on to prove his case by listing out scenes that supported it.

By the end, he seemed to have us all convinced. "Damn," Eric said. "I think you got it."

The meeting started to wind down. Only two inside jokes had been said, but that didn't stop me from drinking two glasses of wine. I was midway through my third when I had to ask a question. It was about something that had been messing with me for a while now, but it really took center stage after everything that had happened with the Midnight Chemist.

"Alright," I said, "Now that we have that figured out,

I just want to ask one question: why the hell do all these books keep reflecting our lives? The fuck?"

The group broke into laughter at my observation.

"Seriously," I continued, "I had to put the book down for the last few weeks."

"I had that same thought," Jess said. She pushed a wave of shiny brown hair over her shoulder. "Let's start reading fantasy next."

"So that a dragon can come and burn my house down?" Noah asked. "No, thank you."

"Or so that a dragon makes you com—"

"Jake," Noah said, cutting off his husband with a slap to the chest.

"Ding, ding, ding," Jess said and clapped her hands together. "I want that dragon to light *me* on fire, not my house."

26

TRISTAN HALL

I LEANED against the clean kitchen counter, my brother's face filling my phone screen. He smiled as blue water reflected down from the aquarium tank that surrounded him. He was in the shark tunnel at the Tampa Aquarium, where he'd found his dream job pretty early on in life. That's something us as brothers happened to share: aside from big smiles and asymmetrical dimples, we'd also both found our passions quickly and worked hard to make our dreams real.

I was proud of him.

"And you're sure everything's good over there?" he asked. I'd just given him the rundown on the most recent developments. My entire family wanted me out of the state, under government protection if possible, so I had to constantly reassure them I was fine.

They didn't know about the abduction... that was something I couldn't really bring myself to talk about yet. I couldn't imagine telling my mom over the phone, my little brother, my dad. They would be completely distraught, hurting for me without me being able to comfort them.

That would have to wait until everyone was together. For now, I gave Malik the SparkNotes version of my ordeal.

"I'm good," I reassured him. I glanced at the clock on the wall. Gabriel was supposed to get home in ten minutes. I already had my surprise all set up for him, which made me wish I could just speed up time and have him home earlier. "Gabe is getting close. I think we won't have to be scared for much longer."

"I hope so, Trist. This shit has me stressed the fuck out."

"Yeah, you're telling me." I walked around the kitchen island, glancing out the window above the sink. It looked out to a dark yard, a tall fence surrounding it. There was an invisible fence that ran along the same length, triggering the cameras and yard lights to turn on. So far, all I saw on the camera were cats, squirrels, and a couple of opossums.

Thankfully.

"How's Farrin?" I asked of my brother's new boyfriend. I met him a couple of months back. He was a good guy, with freckles for days and a puppy-dog look every time he glanced at my brother. It was sweet seeing them together.

"He's doing great," Malik said as a hammerhead shark lazily drifted over his head, a manta ray flying close to its fin. "Got a promotion at work. We're thinking of adopting a pup, so we'll see. There might be a new addition to the family soon."

"Well, let me know. I'll send a few chew toys over. From the guncle."

"Perfect," Malik said. He put his fingers up to his forehead and gave a little salute. "Alright, Trist, call me if you need anything."

"You, too. Love you."

"Love you." We hung up, leaving me with the crackling of the electronic fireplace I had left playing on the television. The sound of a car engine pulling into the driveway and turning off drew my attention. I went out to the living room, wearing only a pair of small black shorts. The lighting was low, and the couch had been moved to the guest room, replaced by a white massage table and crisp white sheets, folded with a plush towel rolled up near the headrest. Candles gave off a faint scent of rain-soaked meadows—at least, that's what the label said. All I could smell was the distinct smell of a blue Febreze bottle.

This was literally the least I could do to thank Gabe, who had rushed into my life at the exact moment I needed him. He never second-guessed his role in protecting me, and he worked diligently to figure out what was really going on. I wish I could pay him, but considering how low my royalty checks had been lately, that wasn't a possibility, which made me even more grateful for him. I had asked how he was getting paid, and he told me Zane had shifted his agency to salaried detectives so clients didn't have to take on the burden.

Still, I wanted to throw all the money and time and energy I had at him.

The locks on the door clicked open. The hinges creaked. A large shadow filled the doorframe, coming into focus as the candle flames shifted back into place after fighting with the sudden draft.

"Holy shit," Gabe said, stepping in. He looked around, those blue orbs glittering, that smile growing. He had a bag in his hand, white with thin gray straps.

I grabbed his hand and led him to the table. "I wasn't joking about me giving great massages." I gave him a kiss, my body fitting flush against his.

"I was just gone for twenty minutes," he said against my lips.

"I work fast."

He chuckled and separated from me, lifting his bag and placing it on the massage table. "Let me give you this first." He opened the bag, an Apple logo on the front. He took out a... laptop? What the fuck?

"I know your laptop right now is struggling. Every time you turn it on, the fan sounds like it belongs on an airplane engine and not on your lap. So, I got you a replacement."

He nudged the box forward. I blinked. Blinked again. The laptop was still there, wrapped up in shiny shrink wrap, the clean white box showing an image of the brand-new computer I could never have afforded.

"That way, you can finally finish that series, and I can find out what happens to Xavier and Brandon."

My head turned to him as if it had been placed on a swivel. "You're reading my books?"

"I, uh, yeah... why? Should I not be?"

More shock slowly filtered through me. "I'm just... I always get self-conscious with people I care about reading my work. I didn't even know you liked reading."

"I didn't," he admitted, those blue orbs shimmering like crystal balls. I half expected to see my future reflected back at me.

Maybe it already was.

"I started reading one of your books on my flight here because I was curious, and I got hooked. I blew through the other three books. I hadn't read that way in years. Not since I was a kid. You've got a really powerful voice, Trist. Use it."

I could hardly believe what I was hearing. The man I'd fallen for had just given me one of the best compliments any author could ever hear.

He fell back in love with reading. Because of me.

I wrapped my hands around his neck and pulled him in for another kiss, this one about fifty degrees hotter than the last. My tongue slipped into his mouth, dancing with his, my hands moving down his back. "How are you so fucking special," I asked. "And how did I manage to get you into my life?"

"By being the target of a psychotic serial killer," Gabe teased.

I laughed against his lips. "Oh yeah, that's right. Almost forgot." My smile fit perfectly against him. His fingers trailed down my back, lighting up my skin with tendrils of flame everywhere he touched.

"Thank you, Gabe. Seriously. Fuck, I don't think I can ever thank you enough."

I hadn't realized I'd started to get teary-eyed until Gabe brushed away a streak of wetness from my cheek. He then kissed the same spot, kissing his way back to my lips.

"You don't have to. Being here with me is all I need."

I managed to separate myself from our kisses, my shorts already beginning to bulge. "I'm going to try with this massage, at least. Go ahead, get undressed. I'll turn around," I said, feigning some modesty, and moved my new laptop to a safe spot on the coffee table.

Gabriel chuckled. Then came the zip of his shorts, the woosh of them falling to the floor, the rustle of his shirt joining the pile. Crackling from the fireplace. The table creaking as Gabriel climbed onto it, his low and gentle sigh as he lay down.

I turned, seeing a sight that should have been preserved in the National fucking Archives.

Gabriel was made up of corded muscles and smooth curves. The rise of his ass was hypnotizing, two perfectly tanned globes of fucking heaven. Like a perfect peach, round and firm and slightly fuzzy. Made my mouth water. And if that wasn't enough, his massive thighs made me think there'd be no better way to die than by getting crushed between them. He had to adjust himself so that his thick dick pointed backward, his sac resting on it, soft and inviting me to run my tongue along it.

I had to resist, already feeling myself getting hard at the sight. I palmed my growing bulge as I connected a peaceful-sounding mix of songs to the speakers. Jingles and chimes and gentle beats filled the space.

"Comfortable?" I asked, running a hand across his firm back, applying gentle pressure around his neck.

"Very," he said, groaning as I already started working out a knot.

"Good. Just relax." I went for the scented oils first, spreading some lavender and rose on my hands. I then held them up under the table by his nose. "Take a deep breath in. That's it." I watched his back swell in the dim light, then watched as his body melted downward on the exhale.

"One more time."

Again, his back rose and fell. The top of his head was right up against my growing dick. I wasn't shy about it, letting it rub against him as I moved my hands up to his shoulders, leaning forward so that I could knead out his muscles. He released another moan, my bulging shorts resting on his head. He was tense, which wasn't entirely a surprise. Gabriel had a high-stress job, and he apparently kept all that stress in his upper body.

"When's the last time you got a massage?" I asked as I moved around the table, switching to a non-scented oil and squeezing a line of it down Gabe's spine. It made him shine under the orange glow from the candles.

"I can't even remember."

"Well, you'll never forget this one. I can promise you that."

"Oh yeah?"

I rubbed the oil down the small of his back, spreading it down over his ass, feeling the tight cords of muscle give way under my touch. "Oh yeah," I said, spreading him open, running an oiled hand between his cheeks. The moan he gave me and the slight arch in his back told me all I had to know about what areas I needed to focus on.

Even though I was the one giving the massage, I was feeling just as relaxed as Gabe. This was my love language, having him lie down while I serviced him, worked his every need, pushed away the tension, and left room for only bliss. I lived for this kind of shit. And the fact that I was doing it with a man who made every day feel like a dream, even when I'd just woken up from a nightmare, made it that much more special. More intimate.

My cock throbbed against the massage table. I squeezed and knuckled my way down his meaty thigh, jumping to the other one before I went down and worked on his calves. As I massaged those, I kept his foot pressed against my hard cock, letting him feel every pulse.

"You know," he said, his voice thick like pouring honey. "It's not fair I'm the only one naked."

"I was trying to be professional."

"Don't worry, I won't tell your boss."

"You sure?" I asked, smirking as I massaged the sole of his foot with my thumbs. I could see that he was getting hard, too, his cock growing thick between his legs.

"Swear. Your secret is safe with me. Go ahead, get comfortable."

I didn't waste another second, dropping my shorts to the floor and kicking them off to the corner of the room. My cock, already leaking, pressed against Gabe's foot. I closed my eyes, bringing his feet together and rubbing them over my rock-hard dick. The song playing over the speakers turned into a mixture of babbling water and wind chimes, mixing with the delicate breaths we were both taking.

I gently set his feet back down and worked my way back up his body, applying more oil as I reached his ass. Here, I pressed myself against him, my cock leaving a streak of precome across his side as I used an elbow to really dig into the muscle.

"Oh shit, Trist, right there. Holy shit." I dug into both solid globes of muscle, using my elbow as a pinpoint of tension, releasing everything he had stored in his body. It was so fucking sexy, feeling him start to squirm underneath me. His body was putty in my hands. I could sculpt him into whatever shape I wanted, and that power made the flames licking up my core even more intense.

I spread him open, running my finger over his sensitive hole. He let out another moan, this one sounding hungrier than any of the others. He arched his back again, inviting me. His body asked for more as he opened for my finger, the oil making it slick enough for me to slide right in.

He gasped as I pushed down, sinking past a knuckle. "Do you ever play around back here?" I asked him, my finger wrapped up in an indescribable warmth. Soft and strong, his inner walls pulled me in deeper.

"Not often, no," he admitted, his voice breaking as I pushed downward.

"Is this okay?" I asked as I applied a little more pressure. His hands went to the sides of the massage table and gripped.

"Yeah, keep going. That feels really fucking good."

I slipped my hand out, defying his ask, but only because I had other plans in mind. There was a black leather case sitting on the coffee table, right next to my new laptop. It was small, discreet. And it had what I thought could send this massage from memorable to blowing Gabe's fucking mind.

"Do you trust me?" I asked him, hand on the case. He lifted his head from the headrest, smiling at me as he looked down at the case.

"I do," he said without an ounce of hesitation.

"Good. Now, put your head back down and relax. It's about to get a lot more intense."

27

GABRIEL FERNANDEZ

I COULDN'T ACCURATELY DESCRIBE how fucking good I felt. Having Tristan's finger inside me was a new kind of paradise. I had to admit that I'd never really fooled around with my ass, and now I could see why I was missing out. It was a different kind of intimacy. My cock pushed down against the table, almost uncomfortably hard. So fucking hard. I wanted Tristan, more than just his finger. I wanted him all.

But it looked like he had other plans in mind. I lifted my head and watched my sexy-as-fuck man walk to the small case, his thick dick swinging between his legs. A flag I wanted planted inside me. It was a sudden hunger that consumed me, made me leak onto the massage table.

Tristan gave himself a slow stroke, smiling as he opened the case. He took out a small purple toy, round with two ends, one noticeably bigger than the other. He pressed a button, and the sound of vibrations filled the room, mixing with the peaceful sounds of a running river.

"Relax," he said, coming back to the table, a gentle hand falling between my shoulders. I laid my head back down, taking a deep breath, my nose filling with the flowery scent of the burning incense. His hand came back down to my ass, spreading me open.

I moaned. Couldn't hold it back. Didn't want to, either. I wanted Tristan to know just how fucking bad I wanted this. I thought back to being in his living room, back in those early stages, when all I wanted was to see him smile.

Now? Well, now I wanted so much more.

His finger brushed against my hole, making me squirm, his hand moving down, rubbing gently over my balls and grabbing my big dick, milking me as he pressed the toy against my ass. I lifted up, giving my cock some space. He put one hand on my hip and put me on my fours.

"God, you're so fucking sexy, Gabe. Fuck." He kissed the small of my back, his grip still tight around my leaking dick. Another moan, another wave of ecstasy. I wasn't used to this, being so exposed. But for Tristan, I'd do anything. Trust was an infinity pool overlooking the Mediterranean between us, reaching out toward the edge of the world. I relaxed as the vibrator pushed past the tight ring of muscle, stretching me open in a way Tristan's finger hadn't done.

"Fuckin' hell, wow," I said, looking back at a practically drooling Tristan, his entire focus on my ass.

"That okay?" he asked.

"Yeah, is it all the way in yet?"

"Not even halfway."

"Fuuuck," I said, arching, giving him even more access. There was a subtle burn that quickly dissipated when another wave of pleasure crashed over me. He pushed it in deeper. I twitched forward, Tristan's free hand on my hip pulling me back. I relaxed around the toy. It filled me in a way I'd never felt before, pushing against my prostate, my balls tightening against me.

"There, it's in," Tristan said, kissing my back, his cock rubbing against my leg.

Fuuuuck. A thought crashed into me in that moment with the force of a runaway freight train.

I'm falling in love with this man. Holy shit.

Maybe it wasn't the right time to think this, or maybe it was the exact right time. A mix of endorphins, adrenaline, oxytocin, serotonin, and all the other happy-as-all-hell chemicals brewing in my veins cemented the thought like a brand against my skin, marked wherever his lips touched, his fingers grazed, his cock dripped.

He turned the vibrator on, and my world unraveled. I collapsed onto the table, the vibrations shaking my very core, the smooth round knob pushing down against my swollen prostate. I gasped, my eyes rolling back. I gripped either side of the table as if I were seconds from floating off into space if I let go.

"Hollllly fuck," I said, even my words coming out with a vibration to them.

"How good does that feel?" Tristan asked, walking around the table and coming to my head, his fingers slowly threading through my hair.

"Incredible. Fuck."

"Good," Tristan said, massaging my shoulders as my guts were being slowly rearranged. I couldn't help but laugh. It was a good one, a disbelieving one.

"Why'd I wait so long to play with my ass like this?"

"Because you waited too long to meet me," he said. I lifted my head, his cock directly in front of my face. I reached for his thighs and tugged him toward me, rubbing him all over my lips. I looked up, smiled, opened my mouth, and let him in. His salty-sweet taste consumed me, my ass still clenching around the vibrator.

Heaven. This was fucking heaven.

I sucked him into my mouth, swirling my tongue and tasting him as if he were the last drink of water in the middle of the desert. Savoring him.

He started to thrust, sinking deeper down my throat. I stretched open my jaw, wrapping my lips around his warm shaft. His fingers threaded through my hair. The sensation of him filling my mouth and the vibrator filling my ass was almost too much. I looked up at him, this sexy, handsome man I called mine, and I felt myself leak onto the table. I'd never been this turned on, this raw, primal. I wanted all of him. I stuffed him down my throat until my nose buried into the soft bush of tight dark curls crowning his cock. I gagged but kept him inside, my fingers digging into his ass. He shut his eyes and held my face down against him until I had to pull back for a gasp of air, saliva connecting my lips to his slick and wet cock.

"Gabe... God, you're perfect. You're everything. Fuck

me, Gabe. I want to feel you inside me while you've got that toy in you. That sound good?"

"That sounds like it'll blow my fucking mind."

"Good," he said, stepping back with a smirk. "That's the point."

I got off the table, the vibrations shaking down my legs. I was so hard my cock was red, pulsing in the air. I had to sink it inside Tristan. Needed to give him my load before I spilled it all over the floor.

"Get on the couch," I said, moving us over to the other side of the room. The warm flicker of orange candlelight made his skin glow, made his eyes look like gems. I reached out and stroked his still-wet shaft, pulling him in for a messy kiss. One that told him all he needed to know.

I needed this.

I needed it.

I needed *him*.

He kissed me back with the same world-shattering force, our dicks rubbing together. I looked down, nearly coming undone right then and there. But I held back. I pushed him down on the couch, his eyes filled with the same blazing hunger I felt as he looked up at me, legs open and cock throbbing.

Yeah. I'm in love.

No denying it now. All that was left was to surrender to it.

I grabbed the bottle of oil and spread it on my cock, being careful not to tip myself over the edge. Tristan grabbed his legs and lifted them up. I helped, hoisting them onto my shoulders, the vibrator still pulsing deep inside me. My knees started to shake. I lined myself up with Tristan's hole, rubbing his stomach as I felt him opening up for me.

I leaned down, taking him into another kiss. He tasted so good. Like a meal I'd been craving for decades. Something that brought me home and to an entirely new universe all at the same time. Familiar and new and all I ever wanted.

I pushed in. We both moaned, my cock spreading him open. I kissed his ankle, working my way up to his feet. I thrust, knowing he could take me.

And he did. His eyes opened wide, but the way his mouth shaped into an O and his eyebrows dipped told me all I needed to know. I held myself there, relishing in the heat, feeling the vibrations in my ass take me to a whole other level. I sucked on his toe, watching as his eyes rolled backward. His hole clenched around me, pulled me in deeper.

I started to rock my hips, back and forth, following a rhythm to an invisible song only the two of us knew how to dance to. He nodded, asking for more without any words. I picked up my pace.

More.

More.

So much more. I slammed into him. Over and over again. His toes curled. My balls tightened as my world funneled in only onto Tristan. No one else mattered. Just us. Forever.

"I'm already so fucking close," I said, feeling myself reach the edge of an impossibly high precipice.

"Do it, Gabe. Give it to me." His eyes turned doe-like. "Please."

"Yeah?" I said between the sound of skin slapping against skin. "You want me to come inside you?"

"Yes, Gabe, please, please. I want it."

"How bad?"

"So bad, Gabe. Oh God. Ohhhhh, fuck."

He started to come, his cock erupting with shot after shot of sticky, sweet release. His ass tightened around me with every blow, pushing me right off the cliff. The sound that rose from my chest resembled that of a caged lion. I unloaded, my thrusts stopping as I pushed myself in deep, painting his guts with my come. My fingers dug into his hips, my mouth going to his ankle, my soul leaving my fucking body and going straight up to gay heaven. The vibrator pushed every last drop of come out of my balls, filling Tristan up to the brim with my seed.

It was ecstasy. Pure bliss. Couldn't describe it, and never needed to. I knew from Tristan's drunken expression that he felt the same exact way, white streaks of come covering his heaving chest.

I pushed in a little deeper, letting him have all of me as I went down for another kiss, not caring that my chest was now covered in his release. If it cemented us together, then all the better.

Breathless, against his lips, still inside him, was when I said it.

"I love you." The words fluttered out of my mouth

like a rush of caged butterflies. His eyes opened wide. His smile grew, and his hands held on to me even tighter.

"I love you, too, Gabe. With everything I've got. You're mine."

"And you're mine."

I kissed him again. And again, and again. Until forever. That's how long I knew we would last, and I was the happiest man on Earth because of it.

I knew in that moment I'd do anything for Tristan. I'd die for him if I had to.

I just had to make sure it never came to that.

28

TRISTAN HALL

THE CROWD slowly filtered into the Fox Theatre—Atlanta's crown jewel for the arts. We sat in the plush velvet red seats, close to the front and toward the center. Gabriel sat on my left, right next to the aisle, while my friends sat in a row to my right. The expansive theatre, with its intricate Moorish architecture and opulent gold accents, had seen its fair share of stories over the years, which made sense for it to host an impromptu book club night. This had been a last-minute decision after Jess got the news from one of her good friends: we had been given *Hamilton* tickets. Apparently, she had been dating one of the producers and brought up the Reading Under the Rainbow book club after a particularly *relaxed* moment.

It worked. She secured us tickets for one of the last nights the show would be playing in Atlanta, a practically once-in-a-lifetime opportunity that none of us wanted to pass up.

We'd meet to discuss the book later in the week.

Which was great, considering I still had to finish reading it. Things felt way too close to home, so I decided to defang the text a bit by hopping on to Google and reading an entire beat-by-beat synopsis of the book.

Turned out Tia was right. The killer was actually the main character. He had taken the victim (whom the reader thought was the killer) to a set of underground train tracks, where he revealed his entire agenda moments before a valiant rescue attempt by the victim's mother. It sounded like a great plot with interesting characters, but could I really be blamed for not wanting to read about a bloodthirsty serial killer?

Nah, I didn't think so.

"Guys want SweeTARTS?" Noah asked, leaning over and shaking the box in front of Gabe and me.

I declined, but Gabriel's hand slipped from mine and turned palm up as Noah shook some colorful treats into his hand. "Thanks," he said, popping them in his mouth all in one go before his fingers slipped back through mine.

Hundreds of little lightning bolts zapped across my skin everywhere we touched, spreading outward. I squeezed his hand, feeling the big fingers with their rough callouses encase my thinner, smoother fingers. I didn't exactly make it my life's mission to hit the gym that often, and typing on a keyboard wasn't the kind of profession that would make your hands weathered and worn.

We were the perfect fit. Two souls that matched in the physical realm, too. And after last night? Holy fucking shit, there was no denying it. Gabe and I were made for each other.

His thumb traced reassuring patterns over my knuck-les, grounding me amidst the booming acoustics of the grand auditorium, made more impressive by the orchestra that played a song I didn't recognize in the slightest but could still get lost in. It helped with the ebb and flow of my own turbulent emotions.

There were moments I felt myself swell on a rush of ecstasy—in *love*. I was in love with the perfect man, and he was in love with me—and then, seconds later, I'd come crashing down to reality, splattering myself all over the concrete. I was being stalked, my life was in danger, he could be in this crowd. Those thoughts were the ones that snatched the air right out of my lungs.

I leaned in and kissed Gabriel's neck. We were in a packed theatre, not a dark alley. I was safe here. I could relax and try to enjoy the night, bask in the glow that still emanated from last night's heartfelt confessions.

Love. Fuck. It had felt so right to say. Like I'd been meaning to say it since the second we met, no matter how messed up the circumstances had been or what kind of guardrails we placed between us. It felt weird to think about, but I guess there was a silver lining to being stalked by a serial killer?

Gabe looked past me, down the row at an empty seat. "And Steven?" he asked.

"Couldn't make it tonight," Eric answered. He looked like an extra-sharp teddy bear, wearing a navy blue sports jacket that made Colton's eyes pop whenever he leaned over.

"I was going to invite Evan," Yvette said as if she

needed to get that confession off her chest. The music from the opera was beginning to reach past the ceiling, signaling the show was close to starting.

"Seriously?" Tia said. She sat in the row behind us with Jess. They both looked like celebrities out on a date in the town. Tia wore a designer leather jacket with a shining eagle on the back and breast, paired with a simple but still-designer black T-shirt underneath. Jess opted for a little more color, her dress a formfitting emerald green that made her look like a walking forest.

Damn. I had some really good-looking friends.

"Yes, I had a moment. I don't like being alone, okay?" Yvette put a hand on her face, shaking her head so that her curls bounced in small waves. "But he's gotten really weird. Kind of aggressive."

"Really? How so?" Gabe asked. His protective streak didn't stop at me; it extended to my friends, too.

As if this man couldn't be any hotter.

"He's been calling me nonstop. And he's started to send letters to my house, but what really made me nervous was that he started sending them to my parents, too. He never even met them. I don't know how he figured out where they live. That's not even the worst of it..."

"What?" I asked, seeing the fear in her eyes magnified by the theatre lights.

"He said he moved somewhere in Midtown to be closer to me. I found him. He moved to Eric's building. He saw him in the elevator just the other day."

"It's fucking weird," Colton said, shaking his head and fiddling with the pearl necklace he wore.

"I'll take a look into it," Gabe said. His jaw was set, hard lines highlighted by a twitch of determination. If he ever looked like a bodyguard, tonight would be the night. He wore a black suit over a black button-up, his muscles nearly ripping through the fabric with any move he made. He didn't wear a tie, instead leaving the top two buttons undone, revealing a thin and tight golden necklace sitting against his tanned skin, a spattering of trimmed hair going down his chest.

"Oh, you don't have to," she said.

"I will. Don't worry about it. He'll stop by Monday."

Yvette put a hand over her chest, her bright red lips curling into a genuine smile. "Thank you."

We sat back into our chairs just as the theatre's grand chandelier dimmed, casting its last glowing aura over the audience. That was also when Gabriel's phone buzzed in his pocket. He took it out and read the message.

I watched the joy in his eyes fade, replaced by a cold steeliness.

"I have to leave, Trist," he said, a note of apology edging his otherwise firm voice. The music was beginning to fade out, the audience breaking out into a loud cheer for the orchestra.

"What happened?" But I already knew. There'd be only one thing important enough to pull Gabe away from my side. "Is it the Midnight Chemist?" I asked, my heartbeat threatening to overpower the clapping and cheering from the crowd.

His silent nod was a confirmation, setting a knot of dread in my stomach.

"Just stay here. Enjoy the show. And when it's over, if I'm not back, I want you to stay with Noah and Eric. I don't want you alone for a single second tonight, alright?"

I could barely put a coherent string of words together. A writer, and I was wordless.

Fuck.

He rose, and with an instinctive desperation, I unfastened my Apple Watch, handing it to him. There wasn't any solid reasoning that made me do it. Maybe all of this shit just made me paranoid as fuck. Made me scared of my own shadow, of sleeping in the dark.

An extra layer of caution wouldn't hurt. "Please, take this. I need to know you're safe. At least with this, I can use the Find My Watch app on my phone to know where you're at."

"Smart." He slipped the watch onto his wrist, his gaze holding mine for an extended beat. "I love you," he whispered, the words a fleeting touch before he leaned down and kissed me. Something about this felt wrong. Like I had slipped off the deck of a steady ship into rough and choppy waters working to pull me under. I wanted to get up and go with him, but his urgency told me this wasn't like the last time I cosplayed as his Watson. The stakes felt higher tonight.

It felt like he had found him. Maybe it would be all over tonight? Maybe I could finally wake up from this fucked-up nightmare and start enjoying my life again, not scared of someone sneaking into my house to watch me sleep.

I turned in my chair, craning my neck to watch Gabriel disappear through the theatre doors.

The curtain rose like a river of crimson red, defying gravity and flowing up to reveal a breathtaking set. I tried to get lost in the musical, tried to not to let my brain draw up the most horrific scenarios possible. But the tension only coiled tighter and tighter in my chest as the minutes ticked by. The divide between the staged spectacle and our reality blurred. This was no performance; our lives were the unfolding plot, and the climactic resolution was inching ominously closer.

Fuck.

29

GABRIEL FERNANDEZ

I KNEW who the Midnight Chemist was.

The text that had dinged into my phone was the one that cracked this entire case wide open. Leaving Tristan physically hurt me, like an invisible cord snapped tight around my gut and tried yanking me backward with every step I took, but I knew he'd be safe in the theatre, and I knew that I couldn't waste any time with this.

I knew who the killer was.

The second I left the theatre, I whipped out my phone and called Zane, the owner of Stonewall Investigations.

"Zane, tell me everything you know."

"I don't even get a hello?" Zane teased with a chuckle. There was a buzzing excitement in his tone.

I laughed, looking up at the cloud-dusted sky.

"I've got a name," Zane said, "for who ordered those glass vials you found in the hide-out."

That was good, but it wouldn't be enough. I already had a name, too. First and last. I needed more.

That's when Zane gave me more. "I've also got an address. This guy bought the vials with a gift card, not realizing it still tracked some of his information."

I wanted to reach through the phone and hug Zane, that's how happy I was. An address could easily lead me directly to the Midnight Chemist.

"What did you get?" I asked over the sound of an angry set of honks as someone dodged rear-ending a parked car by a couple of inches.

"I've got a first name: Marlin. And the address is an apartment building. It's called the Iconic in Midtown. Unfortunately, I wasn't able to get an apartment number, but that's where the vials were sent."

Marlin Brooks, aka the Midnight Chemist.

And the Iconic... that sounded familiar. Extremely familiar.

I'd been there before. Eric used to live there; Steven still did. They were neighbors at one point.

Could that mean...

"Thank you, Zane. I think I've got it from here."

"Do you want me to fly in? I can get on a flight and be there in the next three hours, tops."

I considered it. But that meant more waiting, which meant giving more time for this killer to slip back into the shadows. "You can if you want, but I'm going to start working this lead the second we hang up."

"Wouldn't expect anything less. I'll let you know. Stay safe, Gabe."

"Will do, and thank you. I think this could be it."

"Don't thank me—thank Andrew from the Miami offices. He's the one that pieced things together."

"I'll buy him a drink the next time I see him."

We hung up, but I was on another phone call before I could even blink.

"Hello, you've reached the front desk at the Iconic. How can I help you today?"

"Hi," I said, switching my tone over to friendly and custodial. "I'm sending a package to one of my friends and want to make sure it gets to him. Can you make a note to take extra care when that package gets there?"

"Sure thing," the cheery guy on the other line said. "Name and apartment number?"

"Marlin Brooks. He's in apartment... shit. I always switch the numbers. Apartment 215?"

I could hear a keyboard clicking before the guy answered with a "hmmm."

"Was I wrong?"

"Yeah, I think you mean apartment 134. That's where I have a Marlin Brooks registered under."

"Perfect, yup. I'll be sure to write that down. Thank you."

I hung up before he could respond. A cold sliver of ice slipped down my back, as if someone had trailed a frozen finger down each bump of my spine. It was a vicious dread. I pulled up my contacts list on my phone and started typing out a name into the search bar.

Stev— He popped up before I finished typing.

I tapped his name.

The contact card filled the screen.

His phone number was up top. Directly under it was his address.

The Iconic. Apartment 134.

Steven wasn't actually Steven.

He was Marlin Brooks. He was the Midnight Chemist. He had been inside Tristan's home, shared drinks with his friends, read books and tossed around jokes and sat right there next to Tristan on the couch. Always next to him. Never far. He hadn't shown up tonight. Was he worried I was already on his trail? Was he preparing for something else to happen tonight?

I had to get to him. Maybe I could trick him into meeting with me? He didn't know I'd put the pieces together yet; I could still leverage some element of surprise over him.

For the third time in less than three minutes, my phone was back against my ear, ringing.

Ring.

Ring.

"Hello?"

"Hey, Steven," I said. It was rare I got nervous, especially on the job. I had stomped out those nerves from my time in the Marines. Being able to have a razor-sharp focus sometimes meant the difference between life and death.

But right now? I was nervous as all fucking hell. I couldn't mess this up.

"What's up? Everything okay?"

"Everything's fine. I'm actually planning a surprise

for Tristan this weekend. He's been going through so much I figured he deserves something special."

"How sweet of you," Steven said, the words coming out like dry cinder blocks, falling with no actual warmth behind them.

I know who you are.

"I'm going around and getting one of his books signed by all his friends. I want to show him how important he is to us. Mind if I stop by and get your signature tonight?"

There. I threw the chum out into the water; now to see if the shark took a bite.

"Ah, damn, I'm not home."

"That's fine. I can meet you wherever you're at."

A brief pause. Shit. Had I overextended myself?

"Wait, shouldn't you be at the *Hamilton* show right now?"

I looked up at the blinking marquee, the streets empty now that everyone was seated and enjoying the show inside.

"I stepped out. Had to take a call and figured since you live nearby, I could get your signature and be back before the first act is over."

Another pause. This one wasn't as brief, but I didn't try to fill in the silence. Not when that meant stepping directly onto another landmine.

"Cut the shit, Gabriel. You know, don't you?"

That took me like a surprise uppercut to the jaw. I immediately realized that playing dumb wouldn't get me anywhere. He dropped the friendly singsongy voice he usually spoke in, his words blunt and direct like a hammer to the skull.

"I do."

"I was hoping I'd have longer. Damn."

A confession. I had him. Now I just had to make sure I didn't lose him.

"Steven—Marlin—we can make this easy. You can agree to turn yourself in, and we can put an end to this saga. We can go that route—"

"Or you can get in the car."

Just as Steven spoke, a dark black Honda with midnight-tinted windows pulled up right in front of me. The window lowered, and Steven appeared, leaning over an empty passenger seat, phone against his ear.

I should have known he wasn't far.

"I'm not getting in there," I said, every one of my professional instincts shouting at me to shoot at the tires. If I blew even just one of them out, then he'd have a very difficult time escaping. But the attention gunshots would draw could be detrimental. The theatre would surely get evacuated, which would mean hundreds and hundreds of people pouring out into the street. It would make it easy for him to slip into the crowd and disappear.

"If you do, then I'll come clean."

"You can come clean once you step out of the vehicle," I said.

"What are you so scared of, Gabriel? You're twice my size. I don't have any weapons. I don't have any plan. I just want this all to be over with." He lifted his shirt, patted down the pockets of his khaki shorts. "See, I've got nothing."

"Steven, I'm not getting in that car. Get out now before I have to pull you out." I was getting tired of the games. It had gone on long enough.

"Fine," he said, but instead of getting out of the car, he put it in park and jumped over to the passenger seat. "You drive. Take me to the police station, then. Take out your gun, too. Go ahead."

This felt wrong. What was this guy's angle here?

"Drive me to the police station," Steven said. "I can't do it myself. Please."

He didn't wear makeup tonight. His face looked thin, paler than usual. And the scar on his face was clearly visible. A dark mark against his pallid complexion, just underneath his left eye.

This monster had taken so many lives, had come close to taking Tristan's. I couldn't let him escape. This had to end tonight.

I unholstered my gun and kept it in my hand as I walked around the car, getting into the driver's seat. I took a glance into the back seat, just in case. The Midnight Chemist was known to work alone, but maybe he had picked up a bloodthirsty guard dog I didn't know about. All that was back there were a couple black t-shirts and a sea of black, cracked leather. No growling mutt or masked assailant.

It was just me and Steven.

"I'm sorry," Steven said. I couldn't tell if he was apologizing to me or to himself. He was looking out the window as I slammed on the gas. The police station was only a couple of streets away. I kept one hand tight on the steering wheel and the other holding my gun, the barrel aimed at Steven.

I asked the one question I always did when this moment came. "Why?"

He didn't answer. I reached a red light and wanted to blow right through it but stopped with a screech of the tires.

"Why did you kill those innocent people? Why did you stalk Tristan? Break into his house? Kidnap him? *Why?*" I asked again, firmer this time.

That seemed to do it. The floodgates opened. Steven started to speak in a manic sort of way. The words fell out of him like an uncontrolled leak from a roof sitting underneath a torrential downpour.

"Because I'm broken. I'm fucked-up. I'm twisted, inhuman, snapped. Do you know what it's like being locked in a closet for weeks on end? Pissing and shitting in a cup? I should have been worried about pimples and first kisses and school dances, but instead, my father found out I was gay and made me pay for it. He was raging. A big macho conservative politician now had his worst nightmare sleeping in the room next to him. My stepmom didn't care about anything besides the pain pills my dad fed her.

"First, he thought he could conversion camp it out of me. But the moment I got back was when I met the boy I fell in love with. He was the only person I ever felt some kind of emotion toward. I was in *love*. My dad found the emails and moved me into another school district.

"But the emails didn't stop, and my father's anger spiraled.

"He had enough. I'll never forget the first night he pushed me into the same closet he kept his overflow fish tanks. Locked me in there. Full of clown fish—his least favorite—and the anemones they live with. I stared at them until my eyesight blurred. When I'd get hungry enough, I'd stick my hand in and take out a fish, but sometimes my hand would brush up against an anemone.

"It hurt. Really hurt, but it was a feeling. I was starting to lose my grip on those. So I kept sticking my hand in, finding comfort in the burn, figuring that if the toxins took me out, then so fucking be it. But they didn't. I became immune, and I became obsessed." He rubbed his hands in his lap. I noticed there were hairline scars I'd never seen before, flashing in the passing orange glow from the street-lamps. He must have used makeup to cover those up as well.

"My father was the first person I killed. Poisoned him with the same poison I'd get from the anemones, dropped into his coffee. It became easy after that. I went after other gay people, the ones who were living out and proud. Happy. Something I never got to do. It was jealousy—that was really what made me do it. And I don't regret a single fucking second."

I could hardly comprehend the depravity and darkness that I was hearing. Nothing could excuse Steven for his actions, but this would definitely explain them.

The police station was up ahead. I let myself feel a rush of excitement at picturing Tristan's face when I told him it was done. I'd kept him safe. I'd protected him. And now, no one else would ever feel the same terror Tristan felt. The killer would be locked up behind bars. Over time, Tristan would be less and less frightened of his own shadow. We could live a normal life together. One that wasn't ruled by fear and anxiety and paranoia.

I was stopped at another red light, looking at a defeated Steven wringing both hands in his lap, when the needle plunged into my neck. My eyes bulged wide in shock. A jet of cool liquid shot into my artery, pumped directly up into my brain. I couldn't even get a word out before my tongue swelled. Steven only smiled. His thin lips twisted into a sinister smear across his thin face.

The curtains closed on my vision as I slumped forward onto the steering wheel.

30

TRISTAN HALL

I DIDN'T EVEN MAKE it to intermission. It took me about twenty minutes before I leaned over to Eric and whispered to him that I was running to the bathroom just as Alexander Hamilton was singing about not throwing away his shot. Eric made a move to stand up and go with me, but a quick hand on his shoulder stopped him. I mouthed to him that I'd be quick and ducked out into the aisle. My heart was in my throat as I walked through the empty lobby, finding a corner where I took out my phone and opened up the tracking app.

I wasn't sure what I'd find or what I'd do when I found it. I just wanted to make sure it didn't ping back that my watch was in a ditch somewhere or at the bottom of a very deep lake.

It took a second to locate my watch. The spinning wheel on my screen looked terribly ominous. I half expected a skull and crossbones to appear, the word "DEAD" written in bold red underneath.

The blue dot appeared on a small map. I zoomed in on it.

He was back at my place. Weird. Maybe he had to pick something up? I decided to call him, the ringing only lasting about three seconds before the line went completely dead. Any other calls went directly to his voicemail.

"Hey, this is Gabriel. Please lea—"

I hung up. His gravelly voice, normally a balm toward any burns life inflicted on me, now seemed haunted to me. As if the voice was slightly altered, adding the kind of distant echo that only belonged to a ghost.

I looked back to the doors of the theatre. The streets weren't barren, but they were much emptier than when everyone was still in line waiting to get checked in. I could go back inside, wait until the show was over, try calling Gabe again, and if he still didn't answer, then I could figure something out with Noah and Eric.

Or I could get in an Uber and have them race back to my house. Seeing that Gabe was safe would give me the peace of mind I needed. Maybe I'd even have enough time to rush back to finish the show.

I shot a quick text to Eric so he wouldn't worry. *Stomach's really hurting. Might be a while.*

Minutes later and I was in an Uber. "Don't mean to rush, but if you could be heavy on the pedal, I'd appreciate it."

The driver gave me a nod and a wink in the rearview mirror and pressed down on the gas. I tried calling Gabe again but was greeted by his voicemail. It twisted in my gut. Like a cat had its claws tangled up in my intestines, playing with them like string. This felt wrong. I should have left with him or at least had him tell me more about what he'd found out. I tried imagining him sitting on my couch, researching something on his laptop, smiling at me when I opened the door.

The image flashed, replaced with him on the couch, looking up at the ceiling with lifeless eyes, blood soaking into the pillows from the multiple stab wounds in his chest.

My legs bounced up and down; my hand gripped onto the door handle. I wanted to roll out of the car and run to the house myself. Anxiety and dread boiled inside of me. I started to chew on my nails, down to the quick. Blood blossomed against my skin. It tasted like copper on my tongue. I bit down a little harder. Could this guy not drive any faster?

Finally, *finally*, we made it to my house.

"Stop here," I said a couple of houses down from mine. "I can walk."

Something told me I didn't want his headlights shining in through the living room window. I got out of the car on steady feet, even though my knees had a tremble to them. Butterfly knees was what my grandma called them. Whenever I'd get scared as a kid, my entire legs would start to shake. She'd always teased me, saying that it was just a bunch of butterflies that moved down from my stomach to my legs.

I always asked what they were doing in my stomach in the first place, which would get my grandmother laughing. Her laughter would then fight away whatever childish fears I was scared of.

Unfortunately, she wasn't around anymore to fight away the shadows with her bubbly laugh. It was just me. And this dark street. And the dark houses. And... where was Gabriel's car? He had driven us to *Hamilton* tonight, so I figured he would have driven his car back to my house. But the driveway was empty. In fact, the house appeared to be empty, too. Not a single light was on or window open.

Was he really here? Maybe my watch slipped off before he even left the house. I walked down the quiet street, my heart hammering inside my chest.

There! A flicker of light. As if someone had moved a flashlight across the bedroom window, toward the back of the house.

I could walk in through the front door, but I made a last-minute turn and tiptoed to the fence that surrounded my yard. I took out my keys and silently slipped one into the padlock. *Click.* The heavy fence door swung open, inch by inch. I didn't want any creaks or squeaks announcing my presence. I couldn't exactly say why I was sneaking into my own house, just that it felt right.

My yard, the grass freshly mowed thanks to a very attentive Gabriel, looked just like how I'd left it. No glass on the ground from a broken window or tread marks from someone stepping through it. I still tiptoed my way toward the back door, the one that led into the kitchen. I dug in my pocket for the key, pulling it out as silently as I could, stiffening when the keys jingled together at a decibel level that likely wasn't able to be picked up by anyone further than a foot away.

I broke through the freeze that branched out through my nerves. Closing my hand felt like I was cracking it through ice. I turned the key in the lock and gently pushed open the door.

It didn't creak. Gabriel had sprayed the hinges a week ago after I'd mentioned them sounding like banshees.

I wanted to thank him. For everything. Wanted so bad for him to be waiting in the living room, smile on his face as he wondered out loud why the hell I was creeping through my own house.

A groan from my bedroom confirmed my deepest, darkest, most venomous fears. It was followed by the sound of something cracking and then another groan, louder, more pained than the last.

"He's waking up."

That voice. I recognized that voice—no. It couldn't be.

"Hand me the needle."

"Here."

Someone else was here. With Steven. Holy fucking shit. Steven was in my house, he had a needle, and it sounded like he had Gabriel in pain. He was going to kill him here, right there on my bed. I would have gotten home to a silent house, walking straight to my bedroom, where I'd be the one who discovered a lifeless Gabe staring up at me, never seeing me again.

No. That wasn't happening. No.

No, I thought to myself on repeat as I reached for the

biggest butcher knife I had, sliding it slowly out of the wooden chopping block. Time slowed down to a torturous crawl. Like the minutes ticking by inside of a sterile waiting room, waiting to hear if a loved one had made it through a dangerous surgery. Time could contain such infinite possibilities, and inside of those possibilities were nightmarish things tucked away. My hand gripped onto the handle of the knife as if I were a free climber clinging onto the last purchase of rock I could grab before plummeting down to my death.

Another groan. He sounded more lucid. That's when I heard him speak.

"Fuck you," he said.

Gabriel. He was still alive. I could save him. I could get him out of this.

I was only a couple of feet away from my bedroom door. It was dark, but there was some kind of light source in there. Maybe a phone flash turned up toward the ceiling. Stark, bone-white. Shadows moved across it, flickering into the hallway like spirits spilling out from a portal.

"We aren't those kinds of killers," Steven said. "Now, this dose will keep you with us until midnight. Even if Tristan does find you before then, he won't be able to do anything to save you. Then when midnight hits, we all find new beginnings."

I could see someone close to the door. Not Steven. Smaller in frame, buzzed hair. He didn't look very intimidating. He had to be someone Steven trusted, someone that was in this with him.

Someone I could use as leverage. It was another basic instinct kind of reaction. A lion cub hunting for the first time. A bumble of claws and teeth, except all I had was the butcher knife.

I grabbed the man and yanked him against me. I raised the knife and held it against his throat. Jesus Christ, I was holding a knife against a man's throat. What the hell was happening.

And Gabe, he was there on my bed, in just a simple pair of white briefs, splayed out like a starfish. Just how all the victims were found. He was going to be next.

Holy fucking shit. What the fuck.

The man in my arms wasn't struggling. In front of me was Steven, his face lit up by the ghostly white glow of a phone flashlight. My brain could hardly process what was happening. Shock made my legs turn to cement, which helped keep me from collapsing.

"Tristan... I didn't want you finding out like this." Steven put a hand up in the air, needle glinting in his hand. "Let Mason go."

"Mason?" That name sounded familiar... From the bar. The Mason we had interviewed. The one who said he'd slept with the Midnight Chemist and got away.

"Let. Him. Go."

Steven's face twisted in a way I didn't recognize him. I'd known him for close to a year now, having become good friends with the new guy in Atlanta who wanted some gay and bookish friends. He had been in my house, shared meals with me, had drinks with me.

"Why?" was all I could get out of my dry mouth. I

glanced at Gabe, who seemed to be shaking off whatever drug he'd been given. His eyes were wide and focused on the knife in my hand. He wasn't tied down to the bed. Maybe I could stall long enough for him to be able to get up and help me.

"Because I live with a monster in my chest, and I need to feed it, Trist. I have to. But I chose a way that wasn't as painful as others. It's a mercy."

"It's a mercy to stalk and torture your victims?" I asked. The man in my arms squirmed, but I held him a little tighter, unable to press the knife that close to his skin. I really hoped he couldn't feel me shaking.

"That part is a mercy for me. It gives me a thrill I rarely ever feel. And with you, Tristan, the thrill was something I'd never experienced before. I don't know if it's because we've hung out so much or because you're just that special. But Mason and I, we both fell for you."

I shook my head. "Fucking sick. So the surveillance video? The masked man in my house? That was you or Mason?"

"Me," Steven said. "I snuck into your house easy after I made a copy of your key, and I streamed that video footage to your TV during book club. I thought you'd need comfort, thought you'd come to me for it. But then you went to Gabriel, and I realized both of you needed to be handled."

"But you and Mason?" I asked, slowly inching my way closer to the bed. I had to get to Gabe. That's when a thought struck. A possible miscalculation.

Shit... was Mason a victim in all this? Did I just take a hostage hostage?

"Have an understanding," Steven said. "Right, Mace?"

"Yes," he said, his hands coming up to my forearm and yanking down. The force took me by surprise. I wasn't a fighter; I was a writer. Mason could have sneezed and I likely would have dropped the knife. It fell from my hand and clattered onto the ground and was immediately snatched up by Steven.

A small, distant, far-off part of me felt relieved. No longer did I have to face the prospect of killing a man. Now, all I had to do was face the prospect of the end.

But maybe I could bargain. Maybe I could still get Gabriel out of here.

Mason moved to Steven's side. An arm looped around Steven's waist, his fingers gripping the dirty black T-shirt. My eyes widened. They weren't just sidekicks; they were partners. The bartender had looked so saddened when we had asked him about his murdered boyfriend. "How could you?" I asked, hoping to buy some time. "He killed your boyfriend."

"Steven *was* my boyfriend," Mason said. "We've always been together. Ever since we were kids. We met at a neighborhood New Year's Eve party. Exactly at midnight. We made a promise that we'd meet again at midnight, and guess what happened?"

Steven's face twisted into a grin. He now had a needle full of life-ending toxins inches away from Gabe's exposed thigh with the butcher knife in his other hand, aimed out at me. There was a scar on his face I'd never seen before, painted in broad strokes of bleak white light and pitch-dark shadows. "My dad thought he could keep me from him, but that was always impossible."

"Did you know he was the Midnight Chemist? From the beginning?"

Mason shook his head. "No, I didn't know. But when he told me, I was okay with it. He gave me his reasoning and—" His voice cracked with emotion, like a loud whip in a silent room.

I cocked my head. Something clicked. "No. You weren't okay with it. Not anymore. That's why you gave us Steven's real name at the bar. Because you wanted us to finally figure it out."

Mason's big brown eyes cracked open, like a nuclear explosion had just gone off inside his pupils.

"You did what?" Steven asked, turning on Mason.

"You didn't use that name. Haven't used it in years. I got nervous. They had my *phone*. Who knows what they'd find in there. They were asking too many questions—they already knew I was connected to you somehow. I thought—maybe if they thought I was a victim, too. I didn't think you used that name anymore."

Steven appeared dumb-founded. Betrayed. I considered using this moment to launch my lamp at him. Maybe I could knock him out? But if I didn't, he'd instinctively plunge that syringe directly into Gabe.

Shit. Fuck.

Mason looked like he was on the verge of tears. He

started squeezing on the back of his neck. I must have struck some kind of nerve.

"I'm sorry, I'm sorry, I'm sorry."

Steven shook his head and moved closer to Mason, not noticing that Gabriel looked wide-awake. But that needle. It would be so easy for Steven to get at least half of that dose into him, if not the entire thing. Without an antidote, it would sign Gabe's death certificate on the spot.

But maybe if I distracted him?

Maybe if he injected me with it instead? Only one of us had to die tonight.

Maybe.

"Mason was the one who turned you in," I said, pushing into the gaping wound I had uncovered. "He's the one responsible for what's about to happen to you."

I saw a flash of anger twist Steven's features. The scene appeared as if it were drawn in a comic book, using bold black and white markers to draw out the thick outlines and deep shadows. Gabe twitched. He sat up a little straighter, his eyes dropping to the needle and rising up to the knife, now aimed at Mason's chest.

He was about to act. Which meant I needed to act first. I had to be a hero.

I lurched forward. Someone shouted. A gunshot rang out like a massive boom, a star falling through the ceiling, the sky collapsing. I yelled, fell to the floor, another gunshot. Someone was on top of me, covering me. A strong, warm human fortress.

"I've got you, you're okay." Gabe's voice in my ear,

mooring me to reality. I breathed him in, not caring that my ribs were being squeezed tight.

After a few more seconds, the chaos seemed to calm. Gabe unraveled around me, his weight lifting. I got back up on my feet and turned to the doorway.

"Eric?" I asked, shocked.

And Noah, standing at his side. The two of them looked shaken but relieved. Noah turned on the light, and Eric lowered his gun. Behind me, Steven groaned against the wall, clutching at his bleeding shoulder. Mason helped him apply pressure while Gabe quickly snatched away the needle and the knife.

"When you didn't come back from the bathroom, I knew something was up. Noah reminded me you were sharing your location with us, so we followed you back here." He shook his head, gun still aimed at Steven. "I'm starting to think I need to find new friends. Ones that don't have me using my gun every other month."

Miraculously, somehow, the cheery sound of broken laughter bubbled up from somewhere far, far down in my chest. Noah was already on the phone with the police, Jake and Colton barreling down the hallway and into my bedroom.

Gabe helped me out into the living room, where Tia, Jess, and Yvette were waiting for me. Yvette tossed a blanket over my shoulders, and Jess handed one to a still-half-naked Gabriel. The rest of the night whirred past in a blur. I couldn't tell which way was up and which was down. The cops came and took Mason away in handcuffs while the EMTs wheeled Steven away on a stretcher.

They collected all the toxins and needles as evidence and left me and my friends alone after about an hour or two of rummaging through my house.

"So," I said, looking around at the tired faces of the people I loved the most in this world. "Where y'all from?"

The group broke into a smattering of laughter and smiles, and I knew in my heart of hearts that everything would be okay.

31

TRISTAN HALL

THE SUNLIGHT BEAMED in through the window, shining off the freshly mopped hardwood floors. The clean scent of Pine-Sol filled the living room as Gabriel fluffed up a mint-green pillow, and I folded a fluffy beige blanket, placing it in a messy (but still neat) wicker basket with the rest of the blankets. I looked over at Gabe as he bent down to pick up a rogue sock I had left under the couch. He lifted it in the air and shook it, eyebrow arched.

"Whoops," I said, snatching it from his hand before moving in for a quick kiss.

The quick kiss turned into a heated one, well, pretty quickly. It never failed. Feeling Gabe's hard, muscular body against mine always got my engines revving. I wrapped my arms around him and held him against me, my head on his chest, his heartbeat working a familiar rhythm.

Padam. Padam.

I closed my eyes and let myself drift off on a lazy river of pure love.

God, how I loved this man with every single fiber of my being. He was a part of me, a part of my history and my future. The shit we'd been through was enough to fill up a five-season arc on the wildest soap opera on TV, and somehow, we had made it through unscathed. It was a testament to how we were meant to be, how our happy ever after was always written down in the pages of our story.

Between us, both of us were getting way more excited than a hug usually entailed. I could feel him stiffen against me. If it wasn't for the fact that we were about to entertain guests in our new home, then I'd have dropped to my knees and taken him in my mouth about forty-five seconds ago.

Instead, I reached down and gave him a playful squeeze, kissing his neck and peeling myself off him before we both got carried away.

"I think Noah said he was like five minutes away."

"I can do it in three," Gabe teased, grabbing himself before kissing me again. The doorbell rang, earning a playful eye roll from him. We took a second to cool off before I went over to the door, opening it and seeing a smiling Jess and Tia. They held out two bottles of bright pink rosé, yellow bows wrapped around their centers.

"You guys didn't mention you moved into Mariah Carey's old estate," Jess said, stepping inside with her jaw slack.

"Seriously. I think we had to give a drop of blood just to get through security."

"It's not *that* intense," I say as I grab the bottles and thank them both with hugs. "The retinal scans are a little weird."

Gabe chuckled at my joke. "And that's after I complained to the HOA that the rectal scans were a little too much. Thankfully, they took those out."

"Thankfully? Speak for yourself," I lobbied back with a playful slap to his chest. He smiled, the thin golden necklace I bought for him glinting around his neck.

I'd been on a little bit of a spending spree lately. But after landing a seven-figure book deal and multiple film and TV projects, I allowed myself to splurge a bit. Especially when it came to Gabe. I was so excited I could shower him with gifts, similar to how he'd showered me early in our relationship. Everywhere I looked, I was on the hunt for something I could bring back home to Gabe, like a dragon swooping around for treasures to bring back to my beloved.

It had been five months since everything happened with Steven and Mason. Five long but also lightning-fast months. I had gone through the gamut of emotions, finally settling on somewhere between calm and hopeful. The crippling fear had diminished, although random anxiety attacks were now a permanent part of my life. Coping mechanisms were being learned, but that took time.

With the Midnight Chemist locked up for life behind bars, I felt like I had a whole lot of time left.

Which was perfect because all I wanted to do was spend eternity with Gabe, soaking in our successes and living life the best way we possibly could. The book deal had come out of the blue after going on submission with a passion project of mine that I was only able to complete two months after the ordeal.

It only took a weekend—one of those unicorn moments—for three editors to get back to us. By the end of the day, there were seven publishing houses bidding for rights.

Gabe and I drank a whole lot of champagne that night. And the night after.

We also discussed our future. Gabe was taking time off from work to pursue some other passions: mainly his painting. We had a studio that was covered wall-to-wall in canvases, many of them already done, covered in a blend of oil and water color paint that made the room feel like a mosaic of life.

I loved spending time in there. Watching Gabe paint, truly disappearing into his element. We spent a lot of sun-soaked mornings in there.

Lately though, things had been busier on my end, putting a brief pause on the relaxing mornings. I had to buckle down for a national book tour and press circuit while also working on the next book to make sure this wasn't just a (massive) flash in the pan. We'd bought this house and settled in for the long haul. Sometimes I walked around the new house in complete shock, wondering how I'd gone from questionable plumbing and cracking foundation to imported wood floors and vaulted ceilings that turned our living room into a cozy cavern.

Then I remembered all the shit we'd gone through to get here, and I allowed myself a moment to think, *You know what? We deserve this.*

The doorbell rang. Gabe opened it to reveal four smiling faces: Eric and Colton looking cute in slightly matching green polos and jeans, and Noah and Jake, both dressed completely opposite to each other but still complementing the other perfectly. Noah was in a blue-and-white-striped shirt and Jake in a black V-neck.

"Come in, come in," Gabe said. They stepped in just as Yvette showed up with her new boyfriend, Jamie Thomson, a lawyer in a rival firm who'd wooed her over drinks after he suffered a devastating loss when Yvette mounted a kick-ass prosecution against his client.

The whole gang was here. I gave one big tour, showing off the various still-empty rooms with their gorgeous views of the neighborhood lake, spending a little extra time outside by the pool, the sound of a small water-fall competing with the casual chatter.

When we went back inside, we gathered in the family room, everyone taking out a copy of the book we were reading.

A Dragon's Fall by none other than me. The first fantasy book I'd ever written and the one that made me a national best seller overnight. Now, I was getting together with my best friends and the love of my life to get drunk and play games as we talked about the characters and situations that I'd created.

Life really couldn't get any better, and I couldn't be any luckier.

"Alright, I'll do the honors tonight," I said, opening my book and starting our Reading Under the Rainbow club with Gabe's hand on my knee and my smiling friends surrounding me, my book in their laps.

Luckiest man in the world.

ALSO BY MAX WALKER

Book Club Boys

Love and Monsters

Midnights Like This

The Stonewall Investigation Series

A Hard Call

A Lethal Love

A Tangled Truth

A Lover's Game

The Stonewall Investigation- Miami Series

Bad Idea

Lie With Me

His First Surrender

The Stonewall Investigation- Blue Creek Series

Love Me Again

Ride the Wreck

Whatever It Takes

The Rainbow's Seven -Duology

The Sunset Job

The Hammerhead Heist

The Gold Brothers

Hummingbird Heartbreak

Velvet Midnight

Heart of Summer

Audiobooks:

Find them all on Audible.

Christmas Stories:

Daddy Kissing Santa Claus

Daddy, It's Cold Outside

Deck the Halls

Printed in Great Britain
by Amazon

46179139R00159